A NOVEL OF ARKANSAS IN THE 1840s

SURPRISED BY
DEATH

A NOVEL OF ARKANSAS IN THE 1840s

SURPRISED BY DEATH

GEORGE LANKFORD

BUTLER CENTER BOOKS

Butler Center Books

Little Rock, Arkansas

BUTLER CENTER BOOKS

butlercenterbooks.org

Printed in the United States of America

First Edition, 2009

Library of Congress Control Number: 2008942762

This book is printed on archival-quality paper that meets requirements of the American National Standard for Information Sciences, Permanence of Paper, Printed Library Materials, ANSI Z39.48-1984.

Paperback ISBN: 978-1-935106-08-1   [ten-digit: 1-935106-08-2]

10 9 8 7 6 5 4 3 2

Photographs used in this book are the property of the author or were secured for use in this book by the author.

Book design and cover design: Wendell E. Hall
Page composition: Shelly Culbertson
Acquired for Butler Center Books by: David Stricklin and Ted Parkhurst
Project manager: Ted Parkhurst
Project editor: Claudia Utley

This book is dedicated to the following
departed Independence County historians:
to the founders of the Independence County
Historical Society: A.C. McGinnis, whose
1972 account of this incident is still etched
into my mind, and Wilson Powell, whose
knowledge of Batesville history is embedded
in every page; and to Dr. Dan Fagg, my
colleague at Lyon College, whose book
this should have been.

ACKNOWLEDGMENTS

As is always true for authors, I have accumulated a great load of debts to friends and fellow researchers for help along the way. That is particularly true for a historical study such as this, for it has taken more than a decade, with many trips to archives and many conversations. I am grateful to the staffs at the courthouses in Batesville and Little Rock, Arkansas, Holly Springs, Mississippi, and Alton, Missouri. I have received a great deal of help from various staff people in Special Collections in the library of the University of Arkansas at Little Rock, Special Collections in the library at the University of Arkansas in Fayetteville, the Arkansas History Commission in Little Rock, and, of course, the library at Lyon College in Batesville, especially Kathy Whittenton, interlibrary loan specialist. To all of them I offer my gratitude.

The writing itself has been accomplished largely during my final sabbatical leave at Lyon College and episodically through six years of retirement. Moreover, through the trials of four different versions of this book I have inflicted on several of my friends the task of criticism, and they have cheerfully read it and given me their honest opinions. I offer my thanks to Sandy Barnett, Nelson Barnett, Elaine Lankford, Nancy Britton, Jo Blatti, Annie Stricklin, Sally Browder, David Stricklin, Lindley Weygandt, Larry Malley, and Ted Parkhurst. They deserve no blame for the final outcome, of course, but only my gratitude for their help.

George E. Lankford
Batesville, Arkansas

TABLE OF CONTENTS

Independence County, Arkansas, in 1841

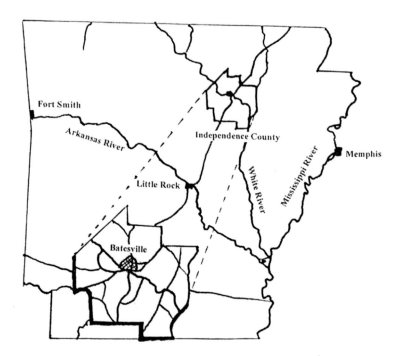

Batesville, Arkansas, in 1841

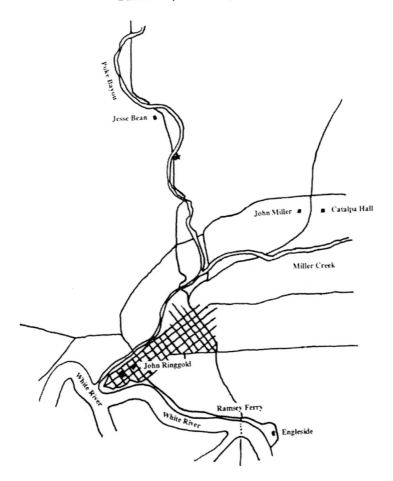

FOREWORD

This book doesn't fit comfortably in any literary genre. It is part historical novel, part fictionalized history, and part fantasy. At its heart it is an account of a "cold case," to use a modern term. It is about a surprising death that upset Independence County, Arkansas, for more than a decade in the 19th century. The drama involved many people and groups of people in the county, and it came to an end only after the major players were dead.

During the life of the drama (1841-1851) and afterward, many people were certain the case was solved, but others had their doubts. The case was officially closed, but it quietly remained an unsolved mystery that no one wanted to re-open. *Surprised by Death* is an attempt to open the files and look again at the "cold case."

The story itself is fascinating, because it introduces the modern reader to a world different from our own. Many ways of doing things, even legal procedures, are alien to the modern world. Officials bent legal rules we think should be rigid, and writers committed libels without censure. Even more provocative than their actions, though, are their ways of thinking. More than a few times the actors in this story demonstrate that they believe notions that we may find incredible or even outrageous.

Perhaps even more interesting to the modern reader than the case itself are the details of life in Batesville, a small antebellum Arkansas town. Images of early Arkansas that we carry in our minds tend to be rooted in stereotypes coded as "frontier," "violent," or just "simple." This story does not offer much support for those images. Instead, tiny Batesville appears self-consciously aware of class structure, from aristocrats to subsistence farmers. There was a wide range of economic security, from impressive wealth to poverty. The people seem obsessed with legal processes and governmental structures, perhaps the result of decades of trying to create a social system similar to the ones they knew back east. Slavery was so much a part of the structure that it was almost invisible in the records, other than as documents of property law. Violence was part of their lives, just as in the modern world, but their concern to control it by religious and legal constraints is obvious in the documents of the time. And "simple?" The tiny world of Batesville is revealed in this story as being extraordinarily complex, participating in the national history in unexpected ways.

Despite all this, though, this book remains a mystery novel. Through my years of reading the materials of the case file, I became unhappy with the original resolution of the story. I have thus provided in this fictional format a fairly accurate account of what happened, as well as my own "solution" to the story. You may wish to read it as entertainment alone, or you may want to be the detective and solve it to your own satisfaction. For those who want to figure it out, a warning: my attempt at a realistic resolution occurs in the last two chapters, so stop reading at the end of Chapter 17 if you want to focus on your own solution.

Apart from the concluding chapters, and despite my fictionalizing of the dialogue and the narrative, the story is historical. These events really happened, and you may end up agreeing with the historian who pointed out that "the past is a foreign country."

George E. Lankford
Batesville, Arkansas

PROLOGUE

Thursday, October 21, 1841

Nick Burton, as is often the case with the young and fit, woke up instantly, filled with energy. He got out of bed and went to the window. As he pulled back the drapes, sunlight flooded the bedroom. It was a wonderful day, just crisp enough to get the blood going. He turned and saw that his brother Phil was still in bed, although he was awake enough to turn away from the burst of brightness.

Nick pulled his nightshirt over his head, splashed some water into the washbowl, and lathered his face and neck with soap and water. The cold water finished the waking process, and when he ran his hand over his face, as he did every morning, the few emerging whiskers reassured him that he did not need to shave for the day ahead. He was fully alert by the time he toweled off his slender body. He pulled his day-shirt on over his head, then tugged on the same pants he had worn the day before. His riding boots completed his costume. No need to dress any fancier for the day's activities, he thought.

He was pleased that his father was sending him several miles north of town to the home of Ben Wilson, the man who was riving out shingles for the roof of their new house. The process was fairly time consuming: oak trees had to be sawed into drums that were then split with the grain with a mallet and froe. Each flat shingle then had to be thinned from the center to one end with a drawknife so that it would fit comfortably beneath the layers above. And it took a lot of shingles to make a roof. Wilson had received the order several months ago, but there had been no contact since. Nick's father needed to be sure that the craftsman was on schedule, because the builders were finishing the frame, and it would not be but a week or so before they would be ready to begin putting the roof on. Dr. Burton had decided that Nick could handle the communication task without help, so seventeen-year-old Nick was looking forward to spending the morning in the saddle, off on a grown-up task.

He crossed to the dresser and pulled a comb through his thick hair. Just a few strokes were enough for him; he looked in the mirror and decided that would do. He considered the ride he was going to make that morning. Despite the date, it was a typical Arkansas fall, with warm days. Nick decided that it was not going to be cool enough for more than his light coat, which he pulled out of the wardrobe and tossed across his shoulder. He went to the foot of Phil's bed and waggled one of the feet outlined under the blanket. "Time to get up, Phil. I'm going on up the bayou. See you."

He turned to the mirror for one last critical look, then was gone.

His father was sitting at the breakfast table, and Nick could hear noise from the room of his sister Nancy. Nick saw food laid out on the sideboard. He said cheerily, "Morning, Father," and went to fill a plate with several biscuits, some ham, and some eggs. The breakfast offerings were more ample than usual, and he suspected it was because he was going on his all-morning journey. He sat at the table.

"Good morning, Nick. Are you feeling well for the ride up the bayou?"

"Of course, Father. Is there anything else that I need to know?" They had discussed his task fairly thoroughly the night before, but Nick thought it was wise to ask.

"No, son. Just be sure that Ben Wilson understands that when the builders are ready to put on the roof, those shingles have to be here. No excuses. If they aren't, I won't pay him.

But find out if he has any problem with delivery. We might be able to help him get them here if necessary, but don't volunteer. Just find out and come back and tell me. And look at the completed shingles yourself—don't just take his word for it."

Nick watched his handsome father as he repeated what he had told him last night. His father was so unbending on things like this, but his threats usually got him what he wanted. Nick, however, knew he would never pass on a threat like that to workmen, especially someone as accommodating and hard-working as Mr. Wilson. "I understand, Father. I'll take care of it." He devoted his attention to his plate, which was soon empty.

As he got up, his father said, "I asked Mary to put something together for your dinner. You just drop by the kitchen on your way to the stable and put it in your saddlebag. Have a good ride."

"Thanks, Father. I should be home early afternoon."

"Don't be much later than that, Nick. Remember that we're going to have supper over at Rosalie's house, and we don't want to be late."

"I'll be here. Don't worry. 'bye, Father." And he was out the back door.

The road he needed to take hardly deserved the name. It went from the north side of the bayou across the wide valley created through many years by the work of Poke Bayou and its smaller tributary, Miller Creek. At this season the road was a track through the dust, but in wet weather it was a muddy nightmare. After two miles it changed character as it moved alongside the bayou into the tree-shrouded narrow valley the stream had carved through the hills. Like so many roads in the region, it was the path of least resistance—travelers took advantage of the streams' work in creating sloping access to the higher stretches of land. In this case, Poke Bayou had been from early settlement the way north both for small boats and for horses. That meant, of course, that every few years the road had to be located anew, because floods routinely wiped out portions of it. The result was that there were always a few significant stumps sticking up high enough in the road to be a problem to wagons and unwary horses, so some vigilance was necessary. Moreover, the dirt road crossed the shallow bayou several times as it followed its path across the wide field, and there was always the danger of a mishap at fords.

Nick decided it was easier—and cheaper—to leave Batesville by going up Main to the path to the ford across Miller Creek, where he would join the road. Off lower Main there was a foot-bridge across the bayou, but still no bridge large enough for horses or wagons, so crossing there would entail a ferry fee. There were not many people heading away from Batesville that early in the morning, so he had the road to himself. It was a beautiful morning, and the autumn leaves were spectacular as he rode across the valley alongside the clear stream that still bore its original name from French days, Poke Bayou. He felt no desire for speed this early, so he was content to let his mare set her own pace. As he rode alongside the bayou he could see a long way across the open fields. In the distance across the bayou to the east he could see chimney smoke from Col. Miller's farm. By the time he reached the border of trees that marked the beginning of the narrow valley where the bayou emerged from the hills, he was feeling very contented.

His mood changed abruptly, however, when he realized that he was riding on the stretch of road that ran past Captain Bean's home where Dr. Aiken lived with his wife Jane, Bean's daughter. He hoped he wouldn't run into Dr. Aiken. Nick's concerns about his father's aggressiveness with people came flooding back to his mind. Poor Dr. Aiken, he thought. He's like a man who has stirred up a hornets' nest and doesn't know which way to run to get away from them. And my father is not going to let him be, he thought. Nick pondered again the sequence of events that had led to his father's current dispute.

As far as he knew, it had begun as a medical issue. Dr. Trent Aiken was a physician who had come to Batesville from Tennessee years ago, or at least a few years before the Burtons, who had moved here just last year. Dr. Aiken was married to

Jane Bean, daughter of one of the earliest settlers in the area, Captain Jesse Bean. He and his family lived right here alongside Poke Bayou in a new house next to Jane's parents' older brick home. He had a wide practice of medicine in the area, and William Byers had been one of his clients for several years. After Dr. Burton came to town last year, Byers and Burton had become friends, probably because they were both Whigs in a Democrat state, but Byers had seen no reason to change doctors. Thus it was that just a few weeks earlier Aiken had been called to see to one of Byers's house slaves, who had a bad pain in her stomach. He had diagnosed it as a liver problem and had placed her on a regimen designed to heal the liver and relieve her pain. Two days later she died.

Dr. Burton had been called to look at her in her final hours, largely because Aiken lived so far from town and the Burtons were just across the street. Burton had offered the opinion to Byers that there was no liver condition and that she had died because of Aiken's erroneous diagnosis. When Aiken later arrived and discovered that his patient was dead and that Dr. Burton disputed his medical treatment, he took offense and entered into a heated debate with Burton. When he heard of the disagreement, Byers gave the two doctors permission to do an autopsy, and Dr. Burton demonstrated to everyone's satisfaction, even Aiken's, that there seemed to be nothing wrong with the woman's liver. Dr. Aiken did not accept Dr. Burton's argument that she could have been saved with a different treatment, and the exchange between the two had grown bitter, with Dr. Burton making public statements about Aiken's incompetence.

The controversy quickly got out into the community, of course, and everybody who was unqualified to have an opinion on the subject had one. Those who had some claim to medical knowledge were wise enough to keep silent. Dr. Daniel Chapman, the other doctor in town, had decided to say nothing, because his support of his colleague Dr. Aiken would be taken by Burton as partisanship against a newcomer, and any support of Dr. Burton could be challenged, fairly, by Dr. Aiken as unwarranted opinion by someone not privy to the facts. A Tennessean, Daniel J. Chapman had been a young physician in Independence County for more than a decade. His wife was Lucretia Jane Sprigg, a sister of Elizabeth Ringgold, who was married to the most important Whig in the area. Chapman, however, was a leading Democrat in Independence County and had run unsuccessfully for state office several times. He knew it would not be politic to take sides between a Whig and a fellow Democrat in this altercation. As a doctor, he kept his own counsel and winced at the disgraceful public display of doctors in dispute. His attempt to get the doctors to make peace had gone nowhere, and each one continued to escalate the public comments about the other's medical knowledge, although it was clear that Dr. Burton was the more aggressive of the two.

Nick sighed. The dispute had continued for days, and people in Batesville and even out in the county had taken sides. Finally Dr. Burton had sent a written challenge to Dr. Aiken. As far as Nick knew, his father had never actually fought a duel, but he had issued challenges before, all of which had either been negotiated away or ignored. In this case, Dr. Aiken ignored the challenge, which left Dr. Burton free to exclaim about the cowardice and dishonor that could be added to incompetence as part of Aiken's character. Aiken took it silently, which made his manliness a topic of common speculation throughout the area. Just last week Dr. Burton had taken the dispute to a new level by publishing and broadcasting a circular denouncing Dr. Aiken both as a doctor and as a man.

For his part, Nick had great sympathy for Dr. Aiken, because, while he did not know him well, he did know his father. It was hard to see how Dr. Aiken could ignore this latest attack and continue to live and practice in Independence County. It might yet turn into a duel, and someone could get killed.

As Nick rode past the turnoff to the Bean home, he could hear the sounds of hammering behind the trees that screened off the house site, but he saw no one, neither white family nor black slave. With some relief, he rode on up the road. It was just a few hours later that he came to the road, really more a two-rutted path, that led up to Ben Wilson's farm on a plateau above the valley. Nick reflected again that he was glad he had been here before with his father, because the little-traveled road was not marked. He took the path and emerged shortly into a clearing in which sat a neat double-pen log house surrounded by outbuildings. Nick noticed that it had an excellent shingle roof, which spoke well for Wilson's craftsmanship. As he dismounted at the edge of the clearing, Nick was relieved to see three large piles of shingles carefully laid up in squares lined up along the fence on one side of the yard. Near them was a two-foot oak drum that had already been split out into wedges preparatory to being split further by the froe. Mr. Wilson was clearly at work on the job.

He hallooed the house, observing the courtesy to see to it that the inhabitants of the isolated house were not surprised. Mr. Wilson emerged from one of the outbuildings. Nick saw no slaves around, so he concluded that Wilson was too poor to own any. It took only a short conversation to make it clear that the shingles could be brought down to Batesville any time, and Mr. Wilson promised to do so. He said nothing about any difficulty in making the wagon delivery, so Nick kept silent about Dr. Burton's willingness to help. After accepting a tour of the farmstead and a drink of cold water from Wilson's well, Nick extended his hand like an adult doing business and was pleased that Wilson responded with a warm handshake, man to man.

After Nick re-entered the Poke Bayou road at the foot of the road to Wilson's house, he rode south toward Batesville for a while, then pulled off to a nearby spring, where he ate part of the dinner he had brought with him. After a short nap in the shade he noted that the sun was past mid-point in the sky. He remounted his horse and set out again. He had gone only a hundred yards or so towards Batesville when he was surprised by a "Hallo" from behind him. He stopped and turned to see a man on horseback approaching him at a nice clip. He recognized him as Bonaparte Allen, a man in his late twenties whom he had met before. He and his wife owned part of the Allen family farm east of Batesville. His sister Eliza was married to Henry Engles, the county sheriff. He was one of the younger generation of Allens who had moved to Arkansas decades earlier and settled near Batesville.

"Mr. Allen," he said as the other man rode up and offered his hand. "We've met before. Nick Burton."

"I remember you well, Nick," he said, shaking his hand. "Call me Boney. Everybody does." Nick smiled at the young man with the stocky build in appreciation of the irony of the name. "Where you going?" Boney asked.

"I'm on my way back home," Nick said. "I've just been up the way here checking on the shingles that Mr. Wilson is making for our new house in Batesville. Where are you headed?"

"I'm going home, too, but I have to stop and pick up some things for my wife in Batesville first. I've been up the road here visiting an aunt of mine who's bad sick."

"Well, let's ride along together," invited Nick. "I'm glad of the company."

Boney Allen had a dark tan on his face and muscular arms, the sign of a hard-working man, Nick judged. That led him to try to carry on a conversation about farming, but as a boy reared in towns he did not know enough for that to last a long time. Boney, though, seemed very knowledgeable. In the conversation he confirmed that he was indeed a hard-working farmer, living close to his brothers and parents on the large Allen family holdings. He had a wife and three children, and they were living fairly well, despite the drought back during the early summer.

With that topic exhausted, Nick wondered whether his controversial father was going to come up, or, rather, *how* Boney was going to raise the questions. As if on cue, Boney said, "My aunt is being treated by Dr. Aiken. You reckon that's safe? Your father doesn't think much of him as a doctor, does he?"

Well, that was smoothly done, thought Nick.

"No," he said aloud, "but I don't know that that means Dr. Aiken's not a good doctor. My father has real high standards. Besides, he kind of likes a good fight."

"You think Doc Aiken killed that darky?" Boney asked directly, looking at Nick for his reaction.

"I really don't know, Boney. It may have been her time to die. I don't know."

"I figure he didn't. I like Doc Aiken, and he looks like a good doctor to me. He sure helped my boy last year, when he had the fever. But I hear that your father's a fine doctor, too," he added quickly.

"I just don't know what to think," Nick said. "Let's talk about something else."

"Sure. Didn't mean to pry. You do much hunting?"

"Yeah, I do," Nick replied with relief at the change of subject. "Deer hunting. How about you?"

And with that, they were off on a conversation that went from deer hunting to bear hunting to coon hunting. Nick shared the remaining ham and biscuits from the dinner Mary had packed for him, but they just ate on horseback and kept on talking. By the time they passed the turnoff for the Bean house, they were talking quail hunting, which Nick had never done. Clearly they had found an area of mutual interest, and Nick was having a grand time talking hunting with a man who had done a lot of it.

The topic might have gotten them all the way back to Batesville, but just a few minutes after they passed the Bean house, a shot rang out. Boney was terrified at the sound, but Nick Burton never heard it. Boney looked up and saw Nick falling from his horse. By the time he hit the ground he was dead.

1
AN ALARM

October 21, 1841

"Nick Burton's been shot!"

The shouted announcement would have stopped the conversation among the men at Spit Corner, but they had already been silenced by the unusual sight of the man on horseback racing down Main Street at a gallop.

"Anybody seen Doc Burton?" the man asked as he reined up. The look on his face was frantic, and the men in the group on the covered porch would later insist that they knew from Boney Allen's wild eyes that Nick was dead.

After a heartbeat's pause, Joe Egner pointed down the dirt street and said, "I saw him go into his office just a short while ago. Is there trouble?"

"Yeah," said Boney. "Nick Burton's been shot. Up the bayou." He paused. "I think he's dead," he added in a voice suddenly hushed. He looked at the gathering helplessly, as if searching for the right words. As his lips opened, he seemed to recall his mission. He said hastily, "Got to find his father," and kneed his horse into motion.

Joe Egner, a merchant who had taken a turn as sheriff a few years earlier, was always decisive. He turned to the gathering and cut through the sudden chaos of conversation. "I'm going. Anybody wants to go, get your horse." He wheeled and saw Bill Hynson's twelve-year-old slave standing transfixed watching Boney race past him. "Dave! Go over to my house and tell Isaac to saddle horses for me and him. Tell him to bring them to me here. Quick, now!" Wide-eyed, the boy nodded and ran past the man whose voice left no room for discussion. He headed toward the Egner house a block up Spring Street.

Egner himself broke into a run and followed Boney down Main to P. P. Burton's office. He got there just as Boney burst through the door and said breathlessly, "Dr. Burton! Nick's been shot."

Burton stopped in mid-sentence what he had been saying to a younger man, and leaped to his feet. "What do you mean, Allen?" Burton cried. "Where's Nick? What do you mean 'shot'?"

"I, I, I … think he's killed. I think he's dead. But I don't know for sure."

"Dead! Who shot him, Allen?" snapped Burton.

"I don't know."

Burton leaped toward Boney and grabbed him by the throat, pushing him against the wall. "What do you mean you don't know, damn you?"

"I didn't see anyone," squawked Boney. "I saw Nick all bloody and ran for my life."

"You ran and left my Nick, you coward? Where did you leave him?"

When he saw that Boney couldn't do any more than gasp, the doctor dropped his hands from Boney's throat and backed away a step. The younger man rubbed his throat as he replied, "Up the bayou road. We were coming down together. Just this side of Cap'n Bean's place there was a shot, and Nick fell from his horse. I came a-running."

"Captain Bean's place!" He turned to the other man, whom Boney now recognized as Burton's son-in-law, Bill Hynson, and said, "Go saddle us some horses. I'll go over and get John Ringgold" Turning back to Boney, he said, "You stay here while I get some help, then you lead us to Nick."

"Yessir," breathed Boney. He sank into a chair and covered his face with his hands. Egner stepped back out of the doorway to make way for Burton and Hynson, each in a hurry with his separate mission. He followed Burton across the street to John Ringgold's brick home.

Ringgold was in his office, but he had apparently not heard any of the commotion. Burton came in the side door without knocking. "John! Get a horse! Is Fent here? Boney Allen just rode in and says Nick has been shot. Let's go!"

Ringgold froze just a moment, absorbing what Burton had said, then said, "Do you have a horse, Burton? Should I get you one?"

"Bill is getting mine."

"Just a moment." He opened the door into the hallway and called, "Fent. I need you." It was only seconds before Fent, sleeves rolled up and collar open, strode into the office.

"Fent, Burton here says Nick has been shot. Let's saddle up."

Fent Noland turned to Burton and grabbed the dazed man by the arm. "Nick has been shot? Where? What happened? Is he all right?"

"I don't know. Up the bayou road. Boney Allen just rode in and said he thought Nick might be dead. We've got to go. Allen will lead us to him."

Fent released Burton's arm with a long shocked breath, and Ringgold took over. "Fent, get our horses. Burton, you go get your horse and your bag. You will need to do some medicine. We'll meet you at Spit Corner. Move!"

At the corner, Ringgold and Noland, on horseback, found a small group of men already there, some mounted, some standing. Egner and his slave Isaac arrived on horseback. Just a few minutes later Burton, Hynson, and Boney rode up. The doctor had his black bag slung over his pommel.

"What happened, Boney?" asked Ringgold.

"I was riding with Nick, Mr. Ringgold. Nick and I came down the Poke Bayou road together, having a good talk. When we got a little past the turnoff to Captain Bean's place, I heard a shot. I saw Nick go flying off his horse, and he hit the ground and didn't move, and there was a lot of blood. I got scared." He looked at the ground. "I was afraid I was going to get shot, too, so I took off to come get you folks to help."

"You left my boy lying there on the ground," snarled Dr. Burton with contempt.

"I ... I'm sorry. I just ran."

"What else could he do, with a gunman there?" asked Fent. "Boney, did you see anyone?"

"No. I took a quick look around as I took off, but I didn't see anybody. I just wanted to get to town as fast as possible."

"Let's ride," Ringgold interrupted. "The others can come along as they get saddled." The party headed up the slope of Main Street at a fast pace. Attracted by the noise, Jasper Blackburn, apprentice at *The Batesville News*, came to the door of the newspaper office just below Spit Corner, just in time to watch them ride off. The sound of their passage brought a few heads to windows and doors, people wondering at the commotion. As the group approached the end of Main Street, where the dirt street became a two-rutter, Fent turned aside to let Burton and Boney get in front, saying "Go ahead to Nick. We'll be along." Noland turned to Ringgold, and said, "John, someone should go for Henry Engles, don't you think?"

"You're right, Fent." He turned to Egner, who had stopped with them, and said, "Joe, would you send Isaac down to the courthouse and see if he can find the sheriff? He might end up having to go to Engleside, but we must have him. Would you do that?" Egner turned to Isaac and asked, "You heard?" The black man simply nodded, turned his horse, and raced back down Main Street toward the courthouse three blocks below Spit Corner.

The rest rode single-file to the ford across Miller Creek, heading for the bayou road. Before the whole group had finished crossing, young Phil Burton, Nick's older brother, had arrived on his horse, having heard the news that was going through town. He was so agitated he was trembling, and when he finally reached the other side of the creek, he galloped off at a pace that outdistanced the others quickly. When he reached his father, he slowed and matched his pace, while the doctor and Boney told him what they knew.

2
WHO'S IN CHARGE?

Thursday, October 21, 1841

Nick was dead.

He lay on his back in the dirt dappled by blood and sunlight. Dr. Burton was kneeling at his side, and the blood on his hands and shirt sleeves bore witness that he had already examined the wounds. When Ringgold rode up and saw him, the doctor had finished, and the father had taken possession. Tears coursed silently down his cheeks as he stared at the handsome pale face of his son.

Despite the wounds in the back of his head, Nick's face was unmarked, except for a slight discoloration on the cheekbone, probably a bruise where he had struck the ground, and for some blood on the eyelids, most likely from Dr. Burton's hand when he had closed the eyes. Nick and his father were surrounded by men who were simply standing and staring in uneasy silence. The only sound was the anguished sobbing of young Phil Burton, who, despite his age, had become a hurt child whose brother had suddenly, violently, died. The blood on his shirt showed that he had embraced the dead boy earlier, but now he sat in the dirt knees up, arms on his knees, head on his arms, weeping.

Ringgold stood by his horse and watched as Fent knelt down by Nick's head and placed his hand on the cold forehead, but whether to ascertain death or to give blessing, Ringgold could not tell. He could see by the look on Fent's face that he was going through his own emotional turmoil. Noland rose and went over to Phil, who leaped to his feet and threw his arms around Fent without a break in his sobbing. Fent held him silently, eyes closed.

It was Noland's response that made Ringgold realize that if anything was going to be done to bring order into the situation, it would have to come from him. The sheriff could be long in coming, he knew. As the town's wealthiest merchant and an important state politician, Ringgold held no office, but was still the man who gave the orders in Batesville. He forced himself to withdraw from emotional involvement in the grieving—there would be time for that. He looked at Joe Egner and found him looking at Ringgold expectantly. There was no sign that he was emotionally incapacitated. As if to give Ringgold a nudge, Egner nodded and said, "What do you think we should do, Mr. Ringgold?"

Ringgold looked at him in relief. "Joe, you've been sheriff before. Why don't you take charge until Sheriff Engles gets here?"

Egner nodded. "Boney," he said authoritatively to the unhappy man standing silently some distance from the body. "We don't know when the sheriff will get here, so let's get busy. This is a crime that needs to be looked into. Show us exactly where you and Nick were, and tell us what happened."

"We came down the road here, and we got to where you are standing," Boney said, pointing to the dusty road now marked by the trampling of many feet. "I think I was talking when I heard a shot. I turned to Nick just in time to see him sort of thrown forward over his horse's neck. He fell on off. His horse shied forward where I could see Nick on the ground. I could see blood all over the back of his head and upper back, so I knew he'd been shot. I thought I might be the next one shot, so I took off down the road." He pointed across the valley toward Batesville. "I reckon that's all I know to tell you."

"Could you tell where the shot came from?"

"No. Behind us, I guess. But I never saw anybody."

"Men," Egner said, "we need to find where the shot came from. We're going to have to know what happened here for the sheriff and the inquest. This is legal business, so we've got to do it right. I want everybody who is able to help"— he cut his eyes at Dr. Burton—"to fan out and look for any sign that somebody was hiding in the bushes in ambush. Let's just start here in the center and move out in an expanding circle. Speak out if you see anything that looks like it might be important."

The group of men had been getting larger as more kept riding up, having belatedly gotten the news and wanting to be of help. They obediently gathered in the center and began walking in an expanding circle, eyes on the ground. Nick's brother-in-law, Bill Hynson, despite his stunned look, was able to join in the search. The Burtons and Fent Noland did not move, maintaining a frozen tableau of grief.

A few moments passed as the circle expanded. "Here!" shouted one of the men. "Footprints over here on the edge of the bank." The men gathered and saw the prints preserved in the dirt, steps leading from the edge of the bank out into the roiled dust of the road, and steps leading back. It was clear to all that a man had walked from the side of the road toward the murder scene and had walked back. The man who had found the prints stepped carefully down the embankment and said, "Looks like he stood here, behind this tree. This woulda been a good place for a shot."

"Look around, men, but be careful. Where'd the man who stood here come from?" challenged Egner. They began to expand their line toward the bayou, but only found two other prints in the wet dirt close to the road. They reached the wet rocks of the streambed and stopped. A moment later, however, one of the men who had ranged upstream called, "Got something!" He turned, holding a piece of paper over his head. Everyone recognized it instantly—they were looking at one of the circulars published by Dr. Burton the week before. The circular attacking Dr. Aiken. They looked at each other, certainty growing in their faces. Ringgold turned his head and looked upstream, toward the home of Trent Aiken, invisible from where they stood.

"Let's get back to the road, men," Egner said, and it was clear from his tone that a decision had been made.

When they had climbed back up to the road, they found Dr. Burton, dry-eyed, talking quietly to Fent and Phil, with the latter mopping his face with his handkerchief. Egner walked up to the group alongside the body and held out the circular. "We found the place where the man stood when he fired, and some footprints into the road and back. A little way upstream we found this. It looks like it's been well read—look at the creases and wrinkles."

He watched realization dawn in Dr. Burton's eyes. "Aiken!" burst from his lips and his eyes narrowed into anger. Egner saw grief being shoved aside by rage, paralysis being replaced with purpose, all within the passage of seconds.

Young Phil Burton was just as quick. "Let's go," he said in a breaking voice. "Let's go get him."

"No," Egner said forcefully. "That's not the way."

"I need a gun," said Dr. Burton. "Who will lend me a gun?"

"No, Doctor!" Egner said again. "This is a matter for the law. You tend to your family. There's time for the rest later."

"Are you going to stand in my way, Joe?" Burton asked belligerently.

Egner was spared an answer, because just at that moment one of the men in the group called out, "Here comes the sheriff!"

The group opened up to face down the road, where Henry Engles and Isaac were riding at a fast clip. As he dismounted, Engles explained that he had been down on the river bank and it had taken Isaac a while to find him. He took in the body of Nick at a glance, then he knelt, rolled the body over on its side, and looked at the bloody wounds. "Buckshot, looks like." He returned the body to its former position and stood. "What can you tell me?" he asked, instinctively turning to John Ringgold.

Ringgold motioned to Egner, who filled him in on their search and discoveries. Engles took the circular and put it in his pocket. He turned to Burton and took his hand. With a deep sadness in his eyes, he said, "Dr. Burton, I'm sorry. We'll find the man who did this, I promise you."

Burton squeezed his hand and said with barely suppressed anger, "We know who did this. You do your duty."

"Be assured, I will do my duty. Now, there will need to be an inquest, and soon. I'm sorry, but you are the doctor on the scene, so we will have to call on you to describe the wounds. In the meantime, you need to go to your family and comfort them. You need to make funeral arrangements. I asked my brother to bring a wagon, because I figured we would need it, one way or another." Joe Egner looked at Ringgold and Noland with a rueful expression, embarrassed that they had not thought of the problem of getting Nick back to town.

"I'll bring Nick's body to your house," Engles continued. "If you will set the time for the funeral by then, I can set the time for the inquest so that it doesn't interfere. Or Mort Baltimore. Mort's the coroner, so I guess it's his call."

He raised his voice to include the whole group, "Right now, I want you all to go back to Batesville. I thank you for your good work out here, but you have done all you can."

"I'll stay with Nick," protested Phil. "I'm staying here."

"No, Phil. Nick doesn't need your help. You have two sisters who need you right now. I'll take care of Nick. I will wait here for the wagon and bring him to you. You need to go home."

As Phil thought about his sisters, tears started from his eyes again. He nodded. Neither he nor Burton had further objections; neither spoke.

"Boney, I'd like you to stay," said the sheriff. "John, Joe, will you stay for a while, too?"

The group moved quietly away, scattering as they found their horses, then riding together slowly back toward Batesville. Dr. Burton, flanked closely by Phil and Bill, rode without speaking. Noland rode behind. Each of the men was lost in his own thoughts, or perhaps just too conscious of the silent Burtons to speak. The community conversations would have to wait until the Burtons had been called away into the separate isolation of the grieving family.

As the noise of the horses died away, Engles turned to Isaac, Egner's slave. "Isaac, would you go down the road and wait for the wagon, then bring it here?" Isaac, who had stood at the edge of the road in silence, glanced at Egner and saw him nod. "Yessir," he said and climbed on his horse.

Engles watched him ride off, then turned to Boney. In a kindly voice, he asked his brother-in-law, "Boney, you all right?" Boney nodded hesitantly, looking at the ground. Engles looked at him for a moment, then turned and asked Ringgold to show him everything that happened after the group arrived. Ringgold walked him around the site, showing him the locations of the footprints and where they had found the circular. Engles asked him for his story, which he gave haltingly.

Bonaparte Allen had spent the night up in Sharp County at his father's request, visiting with his aunt, who was ill. On his way back home this morning he made good time. Shortly after re-entering Independence County, he came up on Nick Burton, who was also heading for Batesville.

"Let's ride along together," invited Nick. "I'm glad of the company."

Boney tried to carry on a conversation about farming, but Nick did not seem to know enough for that to last a long time. Allen talked about himself, told Nick that he had a wife and three children, and they were living fairly well, despite the drought back during the early summer.

With that topic exhausted, he asked Nick about his plans. Nick spoke enthusiastically about the possibility that he might go to sea in the Navy, or that he might even be nominated to attend the Naval Academy at Annapolis. He explained that

Fent Noland was a good friend, and Fent had two brothers in the Navy, so he had written letters on Nick's behalf. Mr. Ringgold had also written to Washington, and Fent's father knew everybody in the national government, and he was going to do what he could.

After they had exhausted their exchange of life stories, Boney asked, "You do much hunting!" And with that, they were off on a conversation that went from deer hunting to bear hunting to coon hunting. By the time they passed the turnoff for the Bean house, they were talking quail hunting. Just a few minutes after they passed the Bean house, a shot rang out. Nick fell from his horse instantly. Seeing that Nick was dead and fearing for his own life, Boney fled to Batesville.

The sheriff rubbed his chin pensively. He looked at Boney and asked, "And you didn't see anyone at all?"

Allen looked down at the ground. "Henry, I was scared. I ran. I saw that Nick was covered with blood, and his eyes were open. He looked dead to me. I looked around real quick, but I didn't see anything, so I put my heels to my horse and got out of there. Next thing I knew I was on Main Street."

Engles looked at his brother-in-law for a moment, then said, "Well..." He apparently thought better of it, and let it drop. He turned to Egner and Ringgold and shook his head. "This is going to be a real mess," he said. "Who would back-shoot this boy?" He looked at the still body on the ground in perplexity, as he heard the noise of the wagon from Batesville coming up the road.

Joe Egner said, "Sheriff, do you mind if I ask Boney a question?" Engles shook his head. "How was Nick was lying when you took off for town?"

"He was on his stomach with his face turned to the left, where I was. I could see the blood all over his shoulders, but I could see his eyes open."

"How did he get on his back?"

"I guess Dr. Burton turned him over when he got here," said Allen with a frown. A sudden thought played across his face. "Do you think he was still alive when I left out?" he asked, horror-struck.

"No. Just checking to see that everything makes sense," said Egner.

Engles looked at Egner with respect. As the wagon rolled up, Engles stopped it with an upraised hand. He motioned his brother Peter to leap down from the wagon. After they explained to him what had happened, they all placed Nick's body gently in the bed of the wagon and covered it with a blanket. They tied Nick's horse to the back of the wagon. Peter got the wagon in motion, and the four others fell in behind as they took the slender body toward a town already moving into shock.

Later that day, the Burton family announced that the funeral would take place at one o'clock the next day. Although Nick would lie in the Burton home for visitation until then, the funeral would be held in the town church, which was only one block up from the Burton house. Originally from Virginia, the Burtons were Episcopalians, and the church was Methodist, but it was the only church in town and was used by everyone who needed a church building. Funerals were usually done in the home of the deceased, or by the grave, but this was different. This was likely to be a well attended funeral, and more than a few words would be said.

Sheriff Engles pressed John Miniken, a respected merchant, into service as the acting coroner. Miniken and Engles decided to meet after the funeral to organize and select a panel of citizens and to decide on who would be called as witnesses. Then they would be able to send out the necessary notices for those chosen to come to the courthouse on Saturday morning. They quietly began to pass the word that the inquest would be held on Saturday morning at nine o'clock and that everyone concerned in the case should be there at the courthouse.

3

THE SHERIFF
MAKES INQUIRIES

Friday, October 22, 1841

Henry Engles was up at first light, glad to be able to leave his bed after a sleepless night. There had never been a crime like this in the two decades of the county's history, and he was not sure what he was supposed to do. As sheriff, he basically maintained order and served the papers that the justice system demanded. It was rare that a sheriff was called on to deal with a murder at all, much less one this horrendous.

This was supposed to be the frontier, and people back east had all sorts of notions about the wildness and violence of places like Arkansas. Despite the images, however, it was a reasonably calm area. The county had only been in existence for twenty-one years. It was only a year younger than the Territory itself. The county seat, Batesville, had sported a two-story brick courthouse from the beginning, and there was now a Greek-columned bank building. Even the very first sheriff, Charles Kelly, had little crime to deal with, Engles recalled. He knew that in his decade in the office Kelly had had little to do with criminals other than drunks, disturbers of the peace, and hog thieves. Most of his work, like Engles's, involved assault and battery and law suits to collect debts. Of course, he reflected, any murderers in this area weren't going to hang around for the law to catch up with them. They were, after all, on the western edge of the United States, and there was a lot of wide open space toward the sunset. For that matter, there was a lot of space in Arkansas. It had been a state for five years, but the population was still small. In his years as sheriff, Engles had never had to deal with a real murder charge. And, he thought, he probably wouldn't ever lay hands on Nick Burton's killer, either.

He sighed, tired from his sleepless night and the thought of the day ahead. He knew that he needed to make good use of his morning. With the funeral at one o'clock, he would need to be clean and ready. He certainly intended to watch the faces of people as they sat through the service, because someone might betray some knowledge. He would be particularly interested in watching Dr. Trent Aiken, since he seemed to be the major suspect. Henry's mother had suggested that he position himself by Nick's coffin and watch carefully as people came to pay their respects. "If the wound starts to bleed," she had assured him, "you're looking at the guilty person." Born in Germany, Hester Engels—she insisted on the original spelling of their name—was well armed with European traditions. Henry had no faith in such notions, however, and he had made only a brief visit to the Burton home last night just to pay his respects. He had seen no sign of blood on the body of young Nick in his coffin.

He intended to go out to the murder scene again and see whether they had overlooked anything yesterday. Then he would visit Jesse Bean's household and see what he and Dr. Aiken had to say. It was curious that no one from the farm, not even a slave, had shown up at the adjacent murder site yesterday. How could they not have heard all the commotion? After that, he would call on John Miller, Jesse Bean's brother-in-law. Those two farms were the closest to the scene. Who knew what someone might have seen or heard? He reckoned those tasks would be about all he could do before the funeral.

Engles saddled his horse and sat on the back porch of his house to wait for Joe Egner. Impressed with Joe's orderly mind in the questioning of Allen at the murder scene, he had asked him to accompany him this morning. They were old friends, since their parents—all from solid German immigrant families who still spoke the language—had immediately struck up a friendship with each other when the Engels family arrived in the area. Henry admitted to himself that he would be glad of Joe's company, because he was in unknown territory conducting a murder investigation.

Joe had said he would meet him at the path at the northeast end of Main Street leading to the Miller Creek ford within an hour after dawn, as soon as he could get away. It was still a bit early, Engles thought, so he sat on the veranda of the house where he lived with his family and his parents. He always found the view up and down the White River from his veranda a balm to his spirit.

The Engels family, led by Henry, had built "Engleside" just a few years before, and it was a magnificent place. It stood on the north bluff overlooking the White River, just below the shoals and about a mile downstream from the place where Poke Bayou emptied into the White River at the foot of Main Street. It was an impressive raised cottage, and the slaves kept it neat. The steep bluff down to the small wharf at the river's edge was slowly being transformed by the slaves into terraces planted with shrubs and flowers. The Engles family, in the good German tradition, insisted on an orderly and efficient house and farmstead. Then, too, Henry reflected, his house was the first sign of Batesville seen by anyone coming upriver on keelboats or steamboats. It was fitting, he felt, that the sheriff's house present an excellent introduction to their little town.

With impatience, Engles realized that he couldn't sit still any longer. If necessary, he would just have to wait for Egner for a while at the appointed spot. He mounted his horse and slipped quietly away into the new day. It took only a few minutes to reach the path heading north to the high ground away from the river. He crossed the new east-west dirt road recently named in memory of William Henry Harrison, who had died earlier in the year after just a few days in the White House.

As Engles reached the top of the slope and started down the northern side, he saw Joe Egner sitting on the ground beside his horse, waiting for him. With a wave and a smile, Egner mounted and the two moved down toward the ford across Miller Creek. On the other side they pulled alongside each other to cross the valley with Poke Bayou on their left. "Who killed Nick, Joe? Any thoughts?" Engles asked.

"I don't know, Henry. This doesn't make any sense to me. Who would kill a seventeen-year-old? How could he have any enemies? Trouble over a woman? He was old enough, I guess. But somebody would know about that. His brother would have told us. Well, that's all I can figure."

"I notice you don't mention the bad blood between the doctors. Dr. Burton seems sure that Dr. Aiken killed Nick." Engles turned and looked at Egner. "Don't you agree?"

"If you hated me enough to want to kill me, would you kill my son? That may seem reasonable when you're reading the Bible, but it doesn't make any sense to me. It would take some kind of madman to do that."

The sheriff did not reply, and they rode in silence for a while.

"You know, Joe, it's easier for me to think of Burton doing that to Aiken's boy than to imagine Trent doing it to Nick."

"Yeah. I agree. I have wondered whether Burton is a little off. It *is* easier to see him as a killer than Aiken. I can see him killing Aiken himself in a rage. I'm not sure about a son, though."

"Maybe he can see himself doing it, and that's why he can blame Aiken. Hmm? What do you think?"

"You could be right, Henry. Whatever makes him believe it, he's going to be hard to keep in line. He's going to cause a lot of trouble before this is over. You watch." Egner nodded to himself, then turned to Engles. "That's all the more reason for us to find the killer, and quick."

"Yeah. Thanks for the 'us,' Joe. I appreciate your help. You've got a good mind for this. Maybe this should have happened when *you* were sheriff."

"No. I had all I wanted of sheriffing as it was. I've got too much other business to worry about," Egner said.

In just a few minutes they rode up on the scene of the murder. They dismounted and walked around the area for a final look. It did not take them long to realize that there was nothing more to be found at the site. The chaotic pattern of footprints in the dust was ample testimony that many curiosity seekers had been there since yesterday, and there was no point in spending more time.

They rode on up the road a ways, then forded the bayou and rode up to the Bean house, noting the elegance of the one-story brick house and the newer frame house nestled in the trees. The houses, with several outbuildings, were surrounded by forty or fifty cultivated acres under good fence, as well as an extensive orchard of fruit trees. Before Engles could halloo the house, he heard the sound of work in the barn. They dismounted and led their horses over to the open barn door, where they heard James, the senior slave of the household, cleaning out one of the horse stalls.

"James," Engles called out, "you in there?"

The black man, who appeared to be about forty years old, looked up. "Sheriff, you come right in. You, too, Mr. Egner." He stood and set down his shovel. He showed no nervousness, but no surprise, either. "What can I do for you?"

"You know about the shooting yesterday?" James nodded. "What can you tell me about it?"

"Well, Sheriff, I don't know nuthin' at all. I didn't hear no shooting myself. I heard about it yesterday afternoon."

Engles caught the "myself" and asked the obvious question. "Did anyone around here hear the shot?"

"Sheriff, I don't know that it be all right for me to be talking to you without Cap'n Bean say it be all right."

"I understand, James. But you need to understand that a killing has been done, and that's way beyond any question of what Cap'n Bean wants you to do. Do you see that?"

"Yes, sir. I do see that. All the same, I'd surely appreciate it if you would talk to the Cap'n first."

"All right. Is he around?"

"I 'spect so. You just go on up to the house."

"Is Dr. Aiken here, too?"

"Oh, Dr. Aiken, he gone."

Engles froze. "What do you mean 'gone,' James?"

"He rode out last night."

"Where did he go?" asked Egner.

"I don't know. And I don't know when he coming back."

Engles felt his jaw clench. "Watch our horses, James."
He turned and strode rapidly toward the front door of the
house. They stopped before the door, where Engles gave Egner
a raised-eyebrow look. He took a deep breath, then knocked
loudly on the wooden panel. It opened so quickly that Engles
knew they had been seen in the yard already.

Jesse Bean stood in the doorway. Engles couldn't read
anything in his face. "Hello, Henry." The older man extended
his hand to Engles, then to Egner. "You the new deputy now,
Joe?"

"Naw, Cap'n. Just keeping Henry company."

Bean looked back at Engles. "Come in. I was expecting
you yesterday evening."

"Today seemed a better time to come, Cap'n Bean. But
maybe not. Is your son-in-law here?"

"No, Henry, he's not. Come on in and let's talk."

They went inside and allowed Bean to lead them into the
parlor. As they entered, Nancy Bean, Jesse's wife, came in the
other door, wiping her hands on her apron. Nancy was a handsome woman, well liked throughout the county. The sister of
John Miller, she had been living in the area since Arkansas was
part of Missouri Territory, before the creation of the county.
The Miller home was just a couple of miles east of the Bean
house. Everyone knew her. She extended her hand to Henry,
who took it with warmth. "Welcome, Mr. Egner," she said,
holding her hand out to him.

"I know why you're here, sheriff," she said. "I'm so sorry
for the Burtons. An awful thing." Engles and Egner nodded
dutifully.

Despite the official nature of the sheriff's visit, she was determined to uphold her sense of hospitality, so she offered them coffee. The two men accepted gratefully. She stepped to the door and gave the order, then returned. "May I take your jackets, sheriff, Mr. Egner?" she asked. When they shook their heads, she sat.

"How's your health, Cap'n?" asked Egner, knowing that no serious questions could be raised until after the coffee was served.

"I'm doing pretty well for my age," Bean responded. "Tell you the truth, though, every morning when I get out of bed I feel that I'm having to pay for all the sins of my youth," he added with a smile. Both Egner and Engles knew that he referred probably not to sins, but to the real events of a warrior's life. Bean's captaincy, unlike most of the military titles in the county, was real, and he could still wield real power. He had fought under Andrew Jackson in two campaigns, and just a few years earlier he had done two years as the commander of a cavalry company, at the specific request of President Jackson. Many of the men from Independence County he had commanded through that tour still lived in the county. Both visitors were careful to show their respect, for they were well aware that Captain Bean could quickly summon a small army to his aid, should he need to do so.

After a few more minutes of amiable conversation about the soldier's life and the aches of aging, they grew silent as a servant came in and served the three men cups of coffee, Nancy declining. When she finished serving and moved toward the door, Nancy rose and followed her. "Well, I know you need to talk, so I'll go back to my work. Tell the Burtons, if there's anything I can do..." Her voice trailed off as she realized the absurdity of the well-worn phrase, given the circumstances. She left the room, shutting the door behind her.

Engles immediately got down to business. "What can you tell me about yesterday's shooting, Captain?"

"Not much, Henry. None of us heard anything, but Trent was down in the field. He came in late in the afternoon and said he had heard a shot. He went looking, and found Nick Burton dead in the road. He said he looked at him and saw there was nothing he could do for him. He figured this was a crime and he'd better not disturb anything, so he left him there and came back to the house to find me, but I was still over at John Miller's house. He sent James's boy to fetch me. By the time I got back, you had gone with the body. I saw the wagon across the valley. Trent and I talked about what the killing meant."

"And what does it mean, Jesse?"

Bean leaned forward and looked intently at Engles. "I don't know, Henry. Trent thinks that Burton will blame him." Bean paused and looked at his clenched hands. "Trent didn't do it, Henry. We all know that, because we know Trent. But we're family, and nobody is going to believe us, unless they want to. And that boy was Burton's son, and you know what Burton thinks of Trent. That doctor's a crazy man. We agreed that it might be best if Trent wasn't here for a while. So he's gone away. He'll be back."

I don't think that was wise, Jesse." The sheriff shook his head. "Dr. Burton does believe that Trent killed his son, and everybody knows about his bad temper. But if other people need a reason to believe Trent shot that boy, you've given it to them. You know what people will say,—'If he's innocent, why did he run?'"

"When Trent gets back, if it comes to it, can you protect him?" Bean asked Engles. "*Will* you protect him?"

Engles's eyes flashed. "I'm the sheriff. *Can* I protect Trent from Burton? I think so. Will I? Damn right I will. Now tell me the truth. Where has he gone?"

"I don't know, and that's the truth. I knew you would be asking, Sheriff, so I told Trent that I didn't want to know where he was headed. I'm not sure he knew. He left out last night, and that's all I know. My wife doesn't know, my daughter Jane doesn't know, the children don't know."

"And none of you can tell me anything about the shooting?"

"No, and that's the truth, too. Although," Bean said hesitantly, "I think some of the servants might have heard something."

"Do I have your permission to talk with them?"

"Of course. But you know they can't testify in court, no matter what they know."

"True enough, but if they know something they can tell it at the inquest. Mort Baltimore's sick, so John Miniken will be standing in for him and will make that decision. He may want you to do the testifying for your slaves. The inquest will be tomorrow morning at nine at the courthouse. If I decide that I want them there, will you see to it?"

"Yes. I need to be there anyhow, to see what is said against Trent." Bean paused for a moment. "Do you think Trent did it, Henry?"

"Jesse, I'll be honest. I'm the sheriff, and it doesn't matter what I believe. I uphold the law. I'll do my job as well as I can, and I'll be fair. But I have to tell you, it looks bad. I don't like this business of Trent running off. Just as soon as you hear from him, tell him to come back. What about you? Are you going to the funeral this afternoon?"

"Yes, we'll all be there, unless you think that's not a good idea. I knew the boy a little, and I'm as sorry as anyone else that he's dead. I can think of a Burton that needs killing, but it certainly wasn't the boy. I don't care much for his father, but I would like to pay my respects to Nick." Engles nodded. *And show the town you have no reason to hide*, he thought, but didn't say.

"I'm going to talk to your slaves now," Engles said, rising. "I'll let you know what I want to do about the inquest."

Engles returned to the barn, where James was still shoveling manure. He had tied up their horses near the watering trough. Working in the other corner of the stall was a young negro boy of about eleven or twelve. James leaned his shovel against the plank divider. "Sheriff, do you know my boy Richard? I was expecting you to come back with more questions, so I called him in here. If Cap'n Bean says it be all right, he's the one you want to talk to."

"Thank you, James. Richard, I'm Sheriff Engles, and this is Mr. Egner. I'm trying to learn everything I can about yesterday's shooting. I want you to tell me everything you know about what happened. Everything. Captain Bean says it's all right for you to tell me what you know."

"Yessuh. I don't know much. I was working out by the bayou yesterday morning. I saw Mr. Nick pass by heading up the bayou road, but he didn't see me. A little time later Dr. Aiken walked by and asked me whose horse he had heard. I told him Mr. Burton, and he went back to the barn and saddled up his horse. He took off up the road, riding fast, looking for Mr. Nick, I guess. After a while a man stopped on the road and axed me where Dr. Aiken had been riding so fast. I told him that he was just looking for Mr. Nick, and he went on. After a while Dr. Aiken come back, but he didn't say nuthin'. He went in the house and got his dinner, I guess. Then Mama called me in to eat, and as I went in, Dr. Aiken, he passed me heading toward the field down there." He pointed south. "He was carrying his rifle. I never seen him again 'til later in the day."

"Did you hear a shot?"

"Yessuh. I heard one."

"When?"

"It was a long while after Dr. Aiken left."

"Did you see him come back to the house?"

"Yessuh."

"When was that?"

"Oh, purty long time after I heard the shot. The doctor went in the house, and after a while he called me over to the door. He sent me to fetch the Cap'n from Col. Miller's house."

"Did you see a body in the road?"

"No, sir. The doctor told me to run through the woods and not go on the road to Colonel Miller's."

Engles was quiet for a moment, thinking. Egner took advantage of the lull and asked the boy whether Aiken had his rifle when he rode back in.

"I don't rightly know, suh. He didn't have it in his hand, but he may have had it on his horse." Egner glanced at Henry.

"Does Dr. Aiken have a shotgun?" he asked the boy.

"Yessuh."

"Did he have it with him yesterday?"

"I don't know. I didn't see it."

"Did you find Cap'n Bean at Colonel Miller's?" Egner asked.

"Yassuh. After a little bit he git on his horse and come on back. I walked along with him. Didn't take us too long, I guess."

"Did you see Mr. Nick's body?"

"Nawsuh. When Cap'n Bean and me got right out there in the valley, we saw some men and a wagon across the valley, but we didn't think much about it. We didn't see no body. When we got to the road right over there across the bayou, we saw lotsa prints and some blood in the dirt, but we went on to the house real quick."

"What happened then?" asked the sheriff.

"The Cap'n tell me to go back to my work. I did. Come sundown, my pa came and got me. He told me that there had been a killin' out there and that I would have to tell what I knew."

The boy didn't seem to know anything more. Engles explained to James and Richard that he wanted Richard to come to the inquest, just in case the coroner wanted to talk to him. As Egner led their horses to the front gate, Engles returned to the house to tell Bean that he would need Richard at the inquest. Then the two men mounted and set out for the Miller household, which was a couple of miles to the east. Col. John Miller knew about the killing, but it turned out that no one on his place knew, or would admit knowing, anything about the events of the day before. Miller confirmed that Bean had been at his house from dinner time on, because they had made a good visit out of Bean's getting witnesses to sign a codicil to his will. He had been there until mid-afternoon, when one of the Bean slaves came running down the lane to tell the Cap'n that he was needed at home.

There seemed to be nothing more to be learned, so the sheriff and Egner headed on back to town. When he let it be known that Aiken had skipped, both of them knew there would be an explosion of gossip in the town. Moreover, Engles thought, when Richard revealed that he had told Aiken about Nick on the road, there would be little further doubt in most people's minds. But he was most concerned about Dr. P. P. Burton's reaction.

4

FAREWELL
TO NICK—I

Friday, October 22, 1841

In his years as a Methodist minister of the gospel, Juba Estabrook could not remember ever experiencing a day as bad as this. A popular young man with a promising future, struck down for no known reason. And not by accident. The death of a young man is hard enough to explain to the grieving. But how do you explain a murder with no reason? How do you even try to make sense of it to a family—no, an entire community— that has been plunged into mourning? And in particular, how could he possibly attempt to minister to Dr. Burton, who was, Estabrook was convinced, mentally unbalanced?

Juba Estabrook looked out over the congregation and thought ruefully that it was a sign of human sin that only stark tragedy could bring this many people into the church at one time. Every seat was taken, and there were many people lined up along the walls. They had opened the windows to allow the large crowd outside to hear. The white clapboard church building, only three years old, had never seen this kind of crowd in its brief existence.

He ran his eyes across the congregation. Everyone he knew in this town was out there. He looked at the Burton family on the front pew. The doctor sat rigid, staring fixedly at the vase of flowers in front of him, perhaps to avoid looking at the open coffin. Nancy sat next to him with her face buried in her twisted handkerchief, and her brother Phil had his arm around her shoulders. He looked as if he were in his private hell, eyes closed and lips quivering as he struggled to keep from joining Nannie in weeping for their dead brother. Next to him was his other sister Rosalie and her husband Bill Hynson. She, too, wept, but she leaned away from Phil as she rested her head on Bill's shoulder.

The other Hynsons sat behind the Burtons on the second row—Henry and Eliza, Nathaniel and Anna. Their children had been left at home in the care of the servants. Bill was the two brothers' connection to the Burtons, but they all had known and liked Nick. As small a group as it was, that was the family present to say farewell to Nick. The other Burtons lived too far away to come to the funeral. All of those in the pew facing the coffin looked distraught and tired beyond relief.

What a reversal of life and mood God had given them, thought Estabrook. This new church building had within this single year seen a joyous marriage ceremony for the Burtons and Hynsons, and now there was a Burton funeral. The Lord giveth and the Lord taketh away. *What must they be thinking?* he wondered, as his eyes moved slowly from face to face, as if to read their deepest thoughts and feelings. Anna Hynson's eyes unexpectedly met his, and he was startled at his instantaneous insight: she would interpret Nick's death as another example of the lawlessness of the frontier, another reason to leave Arkansas and return to what she considered civilized life in Maryland.

Estabrook had no way of knowing that Anna was thinking about that very thing. She was distancing herself from the funeral emotion by recalling her letter to her mother about Bill's marriage three months earlier.

5
ANNA HYNSON'S
LETTER HOME

Sunday, July 27, 1841

"Whoever said that ladies don't perspire had never been to Batesville in July," Anna said aloud as she blotted the drops of sweat on her forehead. Anna Hynson leaned back as far as the straight chair would allow and closed her eyes. Her baby Meddy was taking a nap, so she had maybe an hour to herself. She would like to take a nap, too, but she had vowed last night that she would not let another day go by without writing her mother.

After a few moments of stillness, she breathed a sigh, sat up, and pulled a sheet of writing paper from the drawer of the writing desk. She began collecting her thoughts, as she dipped a pen into the inkwell. What was the news? Billy Hynson's wedding, of course. Her mother would want to know about that above all else. Even if Billy or Henry had written their parents about it, her mother would want to have her own letter. Had anything else of importance happened? Not really. She had written home after Fent Noland's wedding to Lucretia Ringgold, so her mother knew all about that, and she had included in that letter the details of the birth of Henry's new baby, Maria.

Her brother-in-law Henry Ringgold Hynson, now 33, was the oldest of the four Hynson brothers who had come to Batesville from Maryland, and he had been in Arkansas the longest. Henry had arrived in Lawrence County in 1826 and had married Eliza Magness five years later He had enticed his family to join him, first Uncle John and Elizabeth Ringgold, then his brothers. Poor Eliza, she recalled, had not even been able to attend the Ringgold wedding, she was so close to her time. No, there really was not much news, except this awful heat. She leaned forward, dipped her pen in the ink, and began writing.

Mrs. McCall Medford
Chestertown, Maryland

Batesville, Arks.
July 27, 1841

Your letter of the 19th of June, my dearest mother, has remained unanswered much longer than I could have wished, but circumstances have prevented my writing. I received your letter on the 15th,

She paused and looked up, counting the days. "Had it really been that long on the way? Almost a month?" she wondered. Yes, she could see the date of its arrival—July 15—where she had written it on the letter. "Would the mail service ever get any faster? Anything could happen in the time between letters! "By the time Mother gets this letter," Anna thought with a twinge of guilt, "it will have been more than two months since she has heard from us."

just as I had finished my preparations for a party, and was about to dress myself. Since then I have been engaged in getting my house in order and in entertaining the bridal party.

First, and most interesting to you, I will speak of our health, etc., and will then try to give you an account of the wedding. I am well, except that I have suffered from the intense warm weather—I never felt such heat in Batesville. We have had no rain for three or four weeks, and no appearances now favor it. Our streets are so dusty I hate to go out.

"Is that unfair?" she wondered. "Nat says I am too critical of Batesville. Most of the streets in Chestertown are also unpaved. For all I know, they may be having the same awful drought, which means the same dusty roads. Why does it seem so much worse here?"

Mr. Hynson feels the heat very much; Medford also; otherwise they are quite well.

Her twenty-five-year-old husband Nathaniel was another of the Hynson brothers and the most recent arrival to Batesville. He, Anna, and young Medford had arrived in 1839. "Has it only been a little over a year? It seems longer," she thought.

There has been rain in the vicinity of Batesville lately, but before that crops had been much injured by the drought. We have had watermelons, nice-tasted but quite small, owing to the dry season. Our canteloupes, raised from seed which we brought from Maryland, were not as nice as we have had them, but I think that is also owing to the drought.

"It could also be a problem with the soil in the back yard of this rented house," she reflected. If the business went well and they decided to stay here permanently, they would build their own house, and she would have to see to it that the soil was properly prepared for a useful garden.

THE WEDDING

Anna wrote the heading with a strong hand. She loved doing this in her letters, and her correspondents had often commented on it with favor. She felt it reflected the good organization of her mind.

William Hynson was married on the 13th of July.

William, at twenty-three, was the youngest of the Hynson boys to come west. The young bachelor had arrived in 1835 and had lived with his brother Henry's family until after his recent wedding to Rosalie Burton.

*Rosalie, now Mrs. Hynson, was dressed beautifully
in white satin, with blond and pearl ornaments.*

Rosalie Burton was one of the daughters of Dr. Patrick
P. Burton. Originally from Virginia, the Burton family had
moved to Batesville from Holly Springs, Mississippi, only
the year before. William's whirlwind courtship of Rosalie had
resulted in the recent marriage, which had pleased both the
Hynsons and the Burtons.

*She looked very handsome—I think that word
suits her appearance better than any other—her face
is not pretty except her eyes; her form tall and fine
and her appearance altogether very genteel and good.
William was dressed very handsomely though not to
my taste, as he would wear a white satin vest instead
of black, and a colored silk handkerchief, instead of
black.*

Billy—"*Bill*," she corrected herself; he got so irritated when
any of the family slipped and called him Billy—*Bill* actually
had little taste of any kind, and he was under no one's control,
as far as she could tell. He paid little attention to Henry or
Nat, but she hoped that Rosalie would be strong enough to
be the wife he needed. Time would tell. "Bill certainly needs
some guidance, but it would not do to say that on paper," she
thought.

*Miss Nancy Burton and Miss Herrick, a niece of
Mrs. Ringgold's, were bridesmaids. Mr. Phillip Burton
and Mr. Pentecost were Billy's attendants.*

"Should I say more?" she wondered. Nineteen-year-old
Nannie, Rosalie's unmarried sister, was a nice-looking girl,
but Anna could not think of anything particularly interesting
to say about her. Since their two older sisters were married
and had not moved to Batesville, Rosalie and Nannie had
become unusually close friends, even for sisters.

The Herrick girl was just visiting here for the wedding,
and no one knew her at all. She was from a little mining town

in Missouri. Phillip Burton is much more interesting, but if I start in on the Burtons, this letter will turn into a book, particularly if I try to tell Mother about the doctor!

Joe Pentecost was another story, however, but perhaps she should let him wait until another letter. Anna had been curious about the handsome bachelor from Pennsylvania, and she had learned that he arrived with a friend in 1831 on the first steamboat to reach Batesville. The next year the romantic young man had gone as First Lieutenant with Jesse Bean's "Rangers" for their year-long tour on the prairie. She had talked with him at the wedding party, and he told her about his conversations with Washington Irving. Imagine, America's most famous writer on a peace-keeping trip in Indian country with a company of young men from Arkansas! He was now the editor of the *Batesville News*, and she was sure her mother would like Mr. Pentecost. His stories about Irving would show her that Batesville was not as backward as she supposed. "Enough!" she told herself firmly. "This is about the wedding. Organization, Anna."

Charles Hynson could not come.

"Of course not." Always out of step with his brothers, Charles had not found Batesville to his liking. He had moved to the western border of Arkansas and settled near Fort Smith on the Arkansas River. He was too far away to come back for the wedding.

Sophia Ringgold was invited to attend the bride, but her mother objected on account of her youth. She was not thought too young to go to the wedding, however.

A schoolgirl giggle escaped Anna's lips. That was just the sort of catty remark her mother loved in her letters. "But it is true. Thirteen is not childhood, but Elizabeth Ringgold just did not want to be cooperative," she thought.

The entertainment was very good and everything went off well. We gave them a party on the 16th. We sent out general invitations, and many persons were asked here that I would not visit socially.

"Is that too strong? But it's true. Such dreadful people. Mother would be horrified. But they are Batesville's 'respectable society,' so we have to get along with them." She sighed as she dipped her pen in the ink.

> But on this occasion Mr. Hynson thought best to invite all that were respectable, as he wished to be popular. Much offense was given last winter because there were no mechanics invited to Mr. Ringgold's.

By contrast, every craftsman in Batesville must have been at Bill's wedding. Anna much preferred the Fent and Luty's small wedding. "Did I tell Mother about the aftermath of that wedding? I think so. I thought it was quite pleasant, with just the right number of people there. Poor Uncle John thought he was doing the right thing by not making a show of his wealth, but there were many hurt feelings. The life of a politician!"

> Not near all who were invited came, and yet there were more than a hundred here. I was busy for a week, preparing, and had all that I could procure that was nice. We had a handsome meat supper for the gentlemen. Mrs. Henry Hynson assisted me part of the time.

"In fact," she mused, "I would have had a hard time of it if I had not had her help. Eliza is such a dear! And she is so smart about the area—she knows everyone. Of course, she is a Magness, and they have been here forever and are well landed. Henry made a good match."

> I had good servants and plenty of them, and, what was most essential, excellent cooks. I made, with assistance, all my cake and had a quantity of it of different kinds. It was all excellent. The guests seemed to enjoy themselves very much. I do not think I was ever as much fatigued as I was the Saturday after I had got all things put in order again and all the borrowed things sent home.

"I've made my mark in Batesville. It was a great success, and I have passed everyone's tests. You should be very proud of me, Mother. You will be able to read between the lines, I hope."

On Thursday last, William, Rosalie, and all the
family together with her sister, Mrs. Wilson and her
husband, dined with us; also brother Henry's family.

"Did I already explain to Mother that Emily and Mr. Wilson live in Mississippi? I think so. She will understand that this was the first time I had met them. Emily is charming, and I thought it was quite clear that she would prefer to live in Batesville with the rest of the Burtons than in Holly Springs. She seemed a little sad when they left to return to Mississippi."

We should have invited Mrs. Ringgold's family,
but Mr. Noland and William do not speak; therefore,
of course it would not have suited.

"I wonder what that is all about? Everyone does. It happened since Fent's wedding in January, because they were cordial enough then. Of course, Bill can be a little tiresome, but it has to be something more than that. But Fent will say nothing about it, and no one wants to try to raise the question any more. Even Bill watches his tongue—he has given no hint at all, just looks unhappy. It probably has something to do with his *not* having watched his tongue. My guess is that Bill said the wrong thing and Fent took offense. I'd wager Bill said something about Fent's duel, that forbidden subject. I certainly would not like to get on Mr. Noland's wrong side! But what could he have said? Whatever it was, Fent will not even shake Bill's hand or speak, and that makes our social life very awkward. It's probably a good thing for Bill that they are both family, because this will probably pass.

"If it was the duel, somebody needs to talk to Bill and make sure he understands not to mention that unfortunate young man. What was his name? Governor Pope's nephew, anyway." It was a story that everyone in Batesville, and maybe all of Arkansas, knew, even though Fent never mentioned it. In 1830 Fent Noland had published a letter hinting at financial improprieties by the Territorial Governor, John Pope. The governor's nephew challenged Noland. A lot of political friends tried to settle the matter peacefully, but the duel was held in Texas. Fontaine Pope—"that was it!"—received a wound that eventually proved fatal. According to the story, Fent asked for and received Pope's forgiveness, but he found it advisable to leave Arkansas and spent several years in military service before returning. It was a sensitive subject to him. "Well, whatever their quarrel, perhaps I had better speak to Uncle John. He seems to have influence with his son-in-law."

> They were invited to the wedding party, but Mr.
> Noland could not come, as his trunk had not arrived
> from Little Rock, and he had no nice clothes.

"Of course he could not come. No one was surprised," she thought with a smirk.

> Lucretia Noland (everyone calls her Luty) was
> here, and she looked very pretty. She is, I think,
> beautiful, but too pale; she is not in good health,
> she is not as fashionable as some other ladies.
> William, Rosalie, and her sister, Miss Nannie
> Burton, left here yesterday for St. Louis.

"Is that a fair judgment on Lucretia Noland? I think so. She still turns the men's heads when she walks into the room, out of fashion or not.

"How nice for Nannie, to be invited to go along on Rosalie's honeymoon! I wonder what Mother will think of that?" she asked aloud with a laugh.

> They go from here to Cape Girardeau in a carriage
> and from there on a steamboat. They expect to be
> gone about a month. I miss them so much.

"Well, truth be told, I wish I were in St. Louis with them, but it wouldn't do to say that to Mother. Or my husband."

Mr. Hynson went to a camp meeting Sunday. He says that instead of tents they have log cabins, which he thinks much better. It lasted five days.

"Those religious camp meetings are so tedious," Anna reflected with annoyance. The "brush-arbor" tradition was an important part of life in north Arkansas, perhaps because there were so few established churches. With several campgrounds in the vicinity of Batesville, meetings were frequently available, and people of all religious persuasions attended services at them. Nat wanted to go, but she had begged off because of the need to take care of Meddy, and Nat hadn't objected. "Imagine! Five days in this heat and dust to listen to long sermons and visit with everyone in the county. Sometimes I think I have married a stranger." She sighed and changed the subject.

Mr. Hynson sends his kindest love and respect to you and says if the distance was not so great he would send you a barrel of his lime as a specimen. It is everywhere thought much of; it has been noticed in two of the principal New Orleans papers. In the news of the 15th you will see a notice of it; also an account of Billy's marriage.

"Oh, dear. I did it again. 'Billy.' Well, let it stand."

Everyone thinks it is certain to be a fortune when they get it well under way. William's business in St. Louis is to get coopers. Expenses are very great indeed, so if they should not succeed there would be a great loss. William sold half the stock of goods that were sent to Carroll County to a gentleman there who attends to the sale of the goods. Mr. Hynson was at the lime kiln today. He says the lime they have just burnt is better than any they have had.

"I'm so proud of Nat," she thought with a fond smile. "He is so smart. Who would have thought he would turn out to be the kind of scientific person who can do these things? This is such a worry to him, though, because it has taken a great amount of capital. When the lime business makes us rich, maybe I'll believe the move to Arkansas was worth it."

Meddy says he is good and loves his grandmother five bushels.

Anna's father had died before Meddy was born, and her mother regularly hinted that she greatly missed the grandson named for their family. She was not watching him grow up. "That is just the way it is for families who move west. At least I can keep her informed—I must try to do better."

The weather is very warm so you must excuse the scrawl. I have written. Adieu. Accept of my love and believe me your ever dutiful,

Anna M. Hynson

There. Her mother would be delighted to get this newsy letter in about a month. She put down the pen and capped the inkwell. Waiting for the ink to dry, she leaned back with a sigh of relief and closed her eyes. "Maybe I can still get in a few minutes of a nap before Meddy wakes up," Anna thought. "But I probably won't be able to sleep. Oh, this heat!"

6
FAREWELL
TO NICK—II

Friday, October 22, 1841

Juba Estabrook ran his eyes across the congregation. He saw the Ringgolds, the women–Elizabeth and her four daughters—red-eyed from the weeping they had already done at the Burton house and were continuing at the church. With a start Estabrook realized that Lucretia, despite her recent marriage to Noland, was only two years older than Nick. *No wonder she looks devastated*, he thought. He looked around the sanctuary at the other children. The contemporaries of Nick were easy to spot, particularly the girls, because they were all sobbing. He noted Mary Cordelia Hughes sitting with her parents, Isabella Pelham with hers, Maria Redmon with her mother and stepfather, Dr. Chapman, and Susan Bevens sitting with her father's arm around her. All of the girls were weeping or past tears. But their parents brought them to the funeral, he noted with approval. Estabrook sighed as he recognized the harsh grace implied in their mourning. *Now, at least, these young women would be aware that in the midst of life we are near death, and their souls would be the better for it.* He thought of mentioning in the service that this was a last gift from Nick to his friends, but he quickly abandoned the idea as the recalled that this was Dr. Burton's son, and he should not say anything to risk the wrath.

He looked back at the Ringgolds. John Ringgold and his son-in-law Fent Noland were dry-eyed, but sad looking. Estabrook had a special feeling for Noland, because Fent had come to his rescue on that terrible day when he was attacked by Dr. Burton. Even if Noland did indulge in frivolous writing for the national readers of the New York *Spirit of the Times*, he was still a serious young man. If that were not the case, he would not have been elected a member of the General Assembly. His uncouth literary character "Pete Whetstone" was just one aspect of his complicated mind, Estabrook felt certain. *And now*, he thought with sadness, *Noland had nothing frivolous in his mind at all, because Nick had been a special friend to him, almost like a young brother.*

What can Fent be thinking? He peered through his spectacles at the Ringgold pew, trying to read behind the frozen mask of Noland's face. Noland was inscrutable, of course, but Estabrook would have been surprised had he been able to divine that Noland had found a place to hide for the moment. He had retreated to pleasant reminiscences of Nick some weeks earlier to escape his grief.

7

FENT NOLAND'S
HAPPIER TIMES

Monday, September 2, 1841

"Steamboat comin'!"

The high-pitched cry from an excited boy almost a block up the street came through the open window and broke through Fent's concentration on the newspaper in his hands. He smiled as he realized that the boy's sharp ears had heard what his attention to the news had caused him to miss—the faint sound of a whistle as a steamboat had come in to the dock at Engleside a mile down the river.

He felt the familiar flutter of anticipation at the thought of the arrival of a steamboat. It had been only ten years ago that the first steamboat—the *Waverly*—had journeyed this far up the White River, and the citizens of Batesville were far from jaded. The *Waverly*'s arrival began the steamboat era of White River life, as Ozarks farmers became dependent on the river transportation for getting their crops to market, especially cotton. The merchants had expanded their store inventories, and long-distance travel to St. Louis or New Orleans became less arduous. Moreover, many Batesvillians had already invested in the building and running of steamboats on the White and Arkansas Rivers. Just last year, in 1840, the local Whigs had called for national "internal improvements" to make possible steamboat traffic throughout the year, regard-

less of the water level in the river. The arrival of a steamboat
nowadays was still exciting to most people, even if it was an
almost weekly occurrence, because it meant packages, people,
news of the outside world, gossip. Some of the stores would
likely receive new merchandise for sale.

The major interest for Fent Noland was that today's arrival
might bring news from Little Rock. He was eager to hear
about political topics in particular. With President Harrison's
unexpected death and John Tyler's betrayal of the Whig Party
and the principles his supporters had thought he espoused,
anything could happen in Washington. President William
Henry Harrison, the Whig Party's first presidential winner,
had endured a cold, wet March inauguration ceremony and
had fallen ill; a few weeks later he had died. Vice-President
John Tyler became president, but he began immediately to
disillusion his Whig supporters, changing his position on the
national bank. It was an exciting time to be a Whig in America,
if disappointing. Fent was now a passionate Whig, even though
his father in Virginia had been a strong supporter of Andrew
Jackson. Under the influence of John Ringgold, though, as the
opposition to Jackson's version of the Democratic party had
evolved into a separate Whig party, Fent had changed from
a traditional Democrat to a Whig. Now there was talk of
throwing Tyler out of the party, and Fent wanted the latest
news.

Noland was also vitally interested in news of the National
Bank. And in the news from Little Rock itself. With both the
Arkansas State Bank and the Real Estate Bank in increasing
danger of collapse, any news would be important, both to
Noland as a legislator and to Batesville as the location of one
of the two branch banks of the State Bank.

Another topic of the moment was how the Fayetteville
scandal was progressing. The preceding April an embezzl-
ment of $46,000 at the Fayetteville branch of the State Bank
had been discovered. The thief, one of Noland's political
enemies, was the cashier of the branch bank, a position equiv-
alent to John Ringgold's as cashier of the Batesville branch

of the bank. He had apparently embezzled the money and then had skipped town in the midst of the scandal. Everyone was waiting to see how the Fayetteville scandal turned out. Noland was concerned about what effect it might have on his father-in-law and Batesville.

Eager as he was for the news, however, there was no reason to rush for the dock at this point, Fent told himself reasonably. He was surprised that the steamboat had made it as far upstream as Engleside. It was August, after all, and while the recent rains marked the end of the summer drought, everyone hoped, the water level was still low. The White River could be counted on for a deep channel only below the mouth of the Black River downstream from Batesville at Jacksonport. If the steamboat had gotten up to Engleside, the next question was whether the captain thought there was enough water for him to navigate through the shoals above Engleside and put in at the Main Street wharf. It was more likely that he would unload at the plantation dock and wait for new passengers and freight for downstream to come overland from the foot of Main Street. It was only a mile, but it would take some time to accomplish. It would be a while, whatever the steamboat was going to do.

Noland returned to his newspaper, a copy of the weekly *Batesville News* that he had picked up earlier at the *News* office up the street. He opened the second page to the column that bore the local notices and scanned them. He was relieved to see that there was no note about yesterday's altercation. He didn't know whether it was just because it happened too close to the press deadline or whether the editor had decided not to include such embarrassing information about a fellow Whig. In any case, it was better left alone.

He himself had seen it. At the major intersection of town, where Spring Street crossed Main Street on its way down to the bayou a block away, there were two stores that shared the honors as the location for the spit-and-whittle men who sat around talking during the day. Spring Street bore that name because there was a small spring at the edge of Poke Bayou that provided a water source for the town. The bayou, which would have been called a "creek" if the French fur traders had not been in the Ozarks before the English-speakers, ran at the bottom of a deep narrow valley, one that required careful paths down to the water and a ferry across the unfordable stream. Someday there would be a bridge across the Poke, but not yet. The difficulty in crossing over the bayou ensured that Main Street would be the more important of the two streets at the intersection only a short block from the bayou.

That intersection was known locally as "Spit Corner," but it was really two corners. In the mornings the porch-sitters occupied benches outside Day, Williams & Co. on the north corner, protected from the sun. When the sun got past mid-day, they transferred to McGuire's store on the south corner, with its pleasant benches flanking the Spring Street doorway. On chilly days they reversed their strategy.

Yesterday morning Noland had stopped to pass the time of day with several men sitting there at Day, Williams, when he saw trouble brewing down Main Street. Dr. Burton had been in the stable behind the Ringgold house performing a minor operation on one of John's colts and had just washed up when he walked out in front of the house. Doctors were often called upon to do medical practice for animals, for their knowledge made them useful substitutes for veterinarians. Dr. Burton was probably glad for the opportunity to work on a horse, Noland reflected, since he had been competing for patients in Batesville for less than a year.

Noland had seen Juba Estabrook coming up the street from the courthouse square, and immediately sensed trouble. He had heard Dr. Burton, who was always on the edge of anger about something, fulminating about Estabrook. Noland believed that Burton needed a wife more than most men, if only to keep him calmed down, but he had had two wives already, one dead and one divorced, leaving him to rear his large family by himself.

Noland had not been at the first encounter between the two men at a camp meeting back in July. He had been told the story by several people, including Nat Hynson, who had been there. Apparently the 55-year-old Burton, who was always attractive to women, had surrounded himself with several young ladies and was playing the gallant. Juba Estabrook, the Methodist circuit minister, who tended to be excessively righteous, like so many clergy, made the mistake of calling attention to the vanity of people who like to show off young ladies—an error compounded greatly by the fact that he did it from the pulpit. Burton had taken it personally, and had later voiced his displeasure in public. Ringgold, when he heard about it, commented wryly to Fent that it was lucky for Estabrook that he was clergy, because Burton might well have called him out otherwise, and Batesvlle would have been treated to a duel between a doctor and a minister. Noland had no difficulty seeing an explosion about to happen as he saw the lines of convergence of Estabrook and Burton on Main Street, whose paths had not crossed since the incident, as far as he knew. He headed down the street at a fast pace to see what he could do.

Before he could get there, he saw the encounter happen below the Ringgold house. Dr. Burton, still in his shirt sleeves, confronted Estabrook and said in a loud voice clearly intended to be heard by all bystanders: "Sir, you took occasion at a camp meeting to insult me by calling the attention of the whole congregation to me. I call upon you to mind your manners, or by God I will teach you some, clergy or not." Estabrook looked stunned, but was totally speechless when Burton shoved him in the chest. Estabrook backed away in confusion, and Burton, in a fury, spat at him in contempt. John Ringgold had arrived at the spot by that time, followed closely by Noland, and they had stepped in front of Burton and taken him by the arms to lead him into the Ringgold house for calming. Burton allowed himself to be taken away, but the town had talked of nothing else since the incident.

It wasn't the first time that Burton had started tongues wagging. A year ago he had done something similar. Noland had seen that one, too. It had occurred right at Spit Corner in front of the porch-sitters. On that September afternoon a group of men were gathered at McGuire's store, and one of them was Dr. Burton, who had only lived in the county several weeks. There was always a lot of activity at McGuire's, not only because it was a popular store, but also because it was the town post office. On that day Thomas Carter, a justice of the peace from south of the river, was in town, and he dropped in at McGuire's to pick up his mail. As he walked up to the Spring Street doorway, saddlebags over his shoulder, Burton leaped to his feet and stepped between Carter and the door.

"Sir," Burton said loudly, "I understand you have made yourself damned busy in my matters, making statements that are false and blackening my name. What do you have to say for yourself?"

Carter, astounded, just shook his head, at which point Burton raised his cane and struck him twice on the shoulder before Carter could react. Carter pushed in to fight him, getting past the cane, then changed his mind and slipped past Burton through the doorway. Once inside, he unbuckled his saddlebag and pulled out a pistol. Fortunately for the doctor, who was unarmed, Sam Wycough had seen what was happening from the corner and had run into the store through the Main Street door. He reached Carter just as he had his pistol ready to fire and was turning back to the porch. Wycough grabbed his arm and began to talk with him, dissuading him from going further with the affair. Out on the porch, Noland and several others had surrounded Burton and were insistently moving him down the steps to the street. They were finally successful in getting Burton to go to his office, after ascertaining that Wycough and Carter had moved into the back room of McGuire's.

That incident, of course, had resulted in a charge of assault and battery against Burton, a case that was still before the Circuit Court. Yesterday's similar incident would possibly do the same. Whether Estabrook felt it important to file a charge or not, Sheriff Engles was unlikely to ignore the very public encounter, and Burton's aggressive behavior was closer to a criminal problem than a civil one. Noland shook his head at the thought of what the Circuit Court was going to be like when Dr. Burton came up before a judge. Maybe I'll be back in the House in Little Rock when that happens, he thought hopefully. Then his lawyer's mind took over, and he realized that he would have to give depositions in the two cases anyhow, since he was an important witness both times. Noland mused about the peculiar Dr. Burton, who was very much a focus of gossip in Batesville, and probably throughout the county.

Fent had asked Tom Carter what he had done that Burton had found so offensive, and he had learned more than he expected. Carter had picked up some background information about Burton—Holly Springs, Mississippi, after all, was only fifty miles southeast of Memphis, and it was almost inevitable that some local resident like Carter would learn of the events that had led to the Burtons' move to Batesville.

Patrick Philip Burton, born in Virginia in the 1780s, had married Emily Scott, the daughter of Maj. Samuel Scott of Lynchburg. She gave birth to seven children before her death in 1827—Selden, Mary, Nancy, Emily, Phillip, Nick, and Rosalie.

The widowed Dr. Burton then married Mary Shields a few years later. At the time of their marriage the Burtons lived in Bedford County, Virginia, where he owned many acres of land and many slaves. He apparently suffered reverses of fortune and ended up moving to Mississippi for a fresh start. No one in Holly Springs seemed clear on what the problem was, but there were guesses about medical lawsuits, extravagant spending, and even gambling debts.

Carter's informant in Holly Springs told quite a story about the Burtons' life in Holly Springs. Mary Shields inherited a good part of her brother's estate, and that set the Burtons on a good financial footing again. Apparently Dr. Burton's Virginia debts followed him, though. In Holly Springs he had done some questionable financial juggling with slaves who actually belonged to his children, gifts from their grandfather, as well as some land for which he was an estate trustee. Carter thought that everything had come out all right in the long run, but there had been a lot of gossip about Dr. Burton's financial arrangements in Holly Springs. The talk got a new burst of energy in 1837 when Selden Burton, the oldest son, completed medical school. It came out that his stepmother had paid for his education, and in return Selden bought the house and lots in which they were living in Holly Springs, putting the deeds in her and the children's names. Holly Springs onlookers concluded that Selden was setting up the arrangement to provide a home for his family, protected from his father's creditors, and perhaps also from his father's financial lapses. Selden himself did not return to Holly Springs to live and practice medicine.

A few months later his sister Mary Burton married Abram Weaver, and the couple settled down in the house next to her stepmother's home in Holly Springs. Within the next year, her sister Emily married George Wilson, son of the founding editor of the Whig weekly newspaper in Holly Springs. These signs that things were getting better were false, because Dr. Burton's financial difficulties continued. There were court judgments against him in Holly Springs, and he finally gave up his medical practice for lack of patients. A sheriff's sale of some of his land made it clear to the community that the Burtons were in desperate straits. When Mary Shields Burton and her three children by the doctor moved to Alabama for an extended "visit" with her brother, the town knew that Dr. Burton had reached bottom. The separation became a divorce. The Weavers moved to Pennsylvania and the Wilsons were well ensconced in Holly Springs, but Dr. Burton was finished there. No one was surprised, Carter was told, when the remaining Burton household—the doctor, Philip, Nicholas, Rosalie, Nancy, and four slaves—moved away to Batesville for another fresh start, leaving the Holly Springs house to Mary Shields and their young children.

What a sad story, Noland reflected. Carter had probably been telling that background information to local people. If Dr. Burton had heard that he was doing so, it would certainly explain why Burton was so furious. Burton himself had never mentioned any of the story to him or anyone else Noland knew, and he had intimated that he was a widower. Noland had cautiously not mentioned any of his information from Carter to anyone except John Ringgold. Given Burton's temper, possession of such knowledge was dangerous, as Tom Carter had discovered. Besides, he had no way of knowing how much of it was true.

In any case, Noland thought, at least Burton might really get a fresh start, if he could stay calm. So far, neither incident had made the *News*. Talk goes away more easily than does an article in the newspaper. He would like to use the incidents in one of his letters to the *Spirit of the Times*, because it was just the sort of story that his fictional character "Pete Whetstone" would love to tell. But Noland knew better—if he wrote about either encounter, Burton could very well call *him* out. And Fent had promised his father that he would never again fight a duel. Better leave it alone. If Burton would get control of his pugnacious spirit, perhaps these incidents would be forgotten. The sooner, the better, Noland thought.

He wondered what Rosalie and the other children thought about their father's behavior. Of all the children, young Phillip probably most took after Dr. Burton in this way; Noland had seen some stiffening of Phillip's spine at real or imagined slights that other people would overlook. Rosalie and Nannie had a good influence over the doctor, and they needed to get back to Batesville. When were they returning? That took Noland full circle, back to the steamboat. There was a possibility that the honeymoon party would be landing at Engleside. It was about time for them to be getting back from St. Louis.

A smile played across Noland's lips as another thought passed through his mind. The original name for the area immediately around Engleside had been "Napoleon," a label bestowed upon it by the first settler there, Charles Kelly. Fent knew the story of how the county seat was originally placed there at Kelly's home at "Napoleon," but had been changed to the mouth of the Poke Bayou a mile upriver. The new town in 1821 received the unimaginative name of

"Batesville," for James Woodson Bates, territorial delegate who steered the creation of Arkansas. Since he had read law under Bates, Noland found the name honorable. However, he mused, to this day there were those who found "Batesville" too prosaic and used "Napoleon" in their letters back east. He wondered idly whether the mail service would deliver to Batesville letters addressed to Napoleon—there was, after all, another Napoleon downriver close to Arkansas Post. Lost letters would be a fitting punishment for such pretentiousness, he felt. "Wonder if I can work *that* into a Pete Whetstone column?" he said aloud.

"Pete Whetstone" was Noland's literary character. For several years he had been publishing letters in the national sporting press, first under his own name, or "N. of Arkansas," then under Pete's name. To his surprise, the bucolic and outspoken Pete Whetstone had caught on immediately with the national reading audience, and nowadays Pete's appearance in books and journals, especially the *Spirit of the Times* in New York, was eagerly anticipated.

Pete had been born slowly. Racing was important throughout the country, and Arkansas was no different. There were many racetracks in the state, with two close to Batesville. Batesville's race track was just northwest of the town across Poke Bayou. The more important local track was less well known because it was not located close to a major town. Thomas Todd Tunstall, planter, steamboat owner, and horse breeder, had lived in Independence County since 1833, and his investment in horse racing was considerable. He owned an enormous amount of land in the eastern part of the county, from Sulphur Rock to Jacksonport, a town that he founded. His plantation was virtually a town in itself, and it included a race track.

To take advantage of the local enthusiasm for racing, the Batesville Jockey Club was created in 1836, with John Ringgold as president and Henry Hynson as treasurer. The group subscribed to the *Spirit of the Times* as a way of keeping abreast of the racing world. Early that year Noland had written

William T. Porter, editor of the *Spirit*, and that first letter appeared in the March 26 issue. From then on, Noland not only reported on the races around Batesville, but as he traveled around the state racing his own horses and enjoying the sporting life, he regularly reported the outcomes to the *Spirit of the Times*, thus becoming an unpaid sports reporter. His first letter *as* Pete Whetstone was published the next year, in the March 18, 1837, issue.

There was a real Pete Whetstone in Independence County, but Fent's Pete was born completely in Noland's mind. Pete's world was the life of the small settlement in the Arkansas hill country—the yeoman farmer who hunts, raises dogs, and amuses himself by drinking, fighting, racing, gambling, and attending political gatherings. It was that world that Fent had chosen over Virginia when he came to Arkansas and made it his lifelong home. Noland was a slender, aristocratic-looking man who was often ill, yet he was an active man of courage, a hunter, a horse owner and racer, a gambler, a bon vivant. His Pete was very much his alter ego, and Noland was profoundly pleased that the national public had taken to him.

He set aside the copy of the *Batesville News* he had been reading and reached inside a pigeonhole in his desk to pull out a piece of foolscap. Picking up a quill pen, he squinted at the nib and decided that it needed a better point. He took his penknife from the drawer and carefully cut a new point on the quill. He dipped the pen into the inkwell, then wrote across the top of the page, "Spirit of the Times." Below, on the right, he penned Pete's nationally known address, "Devil's Fork of the Little Red," and the date.

"My dear Mr. Editor," he wrote, then sat back to compose the right opening sentence. What had he talked about last? Just racing news, he remembered, as "N. of Arkansas." The readers really preferred Pete, though, with his yarns about everything from horse races to bear fights, including descriptions of Arkansas society from the ballroom to the bar (both legal and liquid). In his letters Pete also managed to skewer the pretentious elite of the frontier state and parody the politics. Of course, nowadays it was hard to stay away from more serious political issues, because the financial situation—trying to run a state banking system with little capital and no regulation in a new state with little income, all at the very time of a national depression—made it difficult to avoid sensitive topics. But the Pete Whetstones of the nation were as concerned about banking and the value of the currency in their pockets as any city dweller, so it was not unrealistic to have him comment on those issues along with horse races. The fact that Pete's comments reflected Whig positions on issues was just because they made good sense, Noland reflected with a smile.

As he gazed blankly out the window up Main Street, his eye caught the movement of someone a block away striding purposefully down the street toward him. He focused and felt a warm glow of pleasure as he recognized Nick Burton. "Good," he thought. "I'd rather talk with Nick than write this letter." Although the market, the courthouse, several stores, some houses, and the riverfront lay farther down the street, it never crossed Fent's mind that Nick might not be coming to see him. In the two years that they had known each other, their brotherly relationship had grown, and each took great pleasure in it. Seventeen-year-old Nick did not even try to hide his hero-worship, and Fent, although flattered, found it understandable. After all, Fent, at thirty-one, had been from Virginia to West Point to Arkansas, had fought his duel and killed his man, had been hunting all over the Ozarks, had been in the Army in Indian country and in the Northwest, had carried the Arkansas Constitution to Washington to claim statehood, had been a member of the Arkansas House of Representatives for the five years since then, and had married the beautiful Lucretia Ringgold just a few months ago. He was a friend of Sam Houston, Andrew Jackson, and other notables. What young man wouldn't find such a person fascinating? For his part, Fent, without ever trying to articulate it to Nick, found in him a replacement for his little brother Cal, whom he had rarely seen since leaving Virginia for West Point when he was thirteen.

Fent watched the slender youth walk down the dusty street and was pleased to see how comfortable the boy was with his developing adult body. He would turn out to be a good sportsman, maybe even a good horseman, Fent was certain, and it was already obvious that he had inherited the Burton good looks. Nick was a town favorite, and most people who knew him were already anticipating a good future for him. Fent and John Ringgold had recently written some letters to Washington for him, and it was anticipated that Nick would receive a berth in the Navy, a good beginning for what could become a fine career in military life or in politics. Although, Fent mused wryly, why letters from a West Point dropout should carry any weight, was a wonder.

Nick, as expected, veered toward the brick house. He spied Fent through the window and shouted, "Fent! Fent!"

"Come on in, Nick," Noland said through the open window, motioning to the front hall behind him. While Nick leaped up the four stone steps from the dusty street to the small yard, then the steps before the front door, Fent wiped the ink from his quill and dropped it in the tray, then capped the inkwell. He left the paper lying on the desk. Pete would have to wait. He rose and went toward the front hall, just as the front door opened and Nick entered with a rush.

"Fent! They're back!" he exclaimed with the unrestrained enthusiasm of the young.

"Who's back, Nick?" asked a pleasant voice from the room across the hall from Noland's office. Luty Noland rose from the chair by the front window in which she had been sitting to get the light on her embroidery work, and from which she had seen Nick approach. She walked to the door to the hall, embroidery hoop in hand. "Who's back?"

"Why, Rosalie and Bill," he said. "And Nannie," he added as an afterthought. "They got off the *Franklin* at 'Engleside.' The captain didn't want to come any higher up the river, so they got off there. Father has already sent the wagon for them."

"Where are they going, Nick?" asked Luty.

"To our house for now. Father is there, and Rosalie and Nannie will want to see him first," Nick explained. "I'll bet they've got lots to tell about St. Louis. Henry said he wants to hear right off whether Bill has made some good business investments, and ..." Nick trailed off as he spotted the thinning of Fent's lips, belatedly remembering that Fent and Nick's new brother-in-law were having some kind of dispute.

"Fent, remember your promise to Father," pleaded Luty, who had also noticed the slight movement.

Noland, of course, well remembered his promise to Ringgold to heal the breach between young Bill Hynson and himself. "At least act civilly to each other, if nothing better, so we can all get along socially," Ringgold had urged. They were all well aware that the rift between the two had caused serious difficulties in the party-planning at the time of Rosalie's wedding. The Nolands had not even been invited to one of the Hynson dinners because of it. And John was right, of course, as always. Noland had to make some kind of amends. It was too small a town to carry on public disputes within a family. The whole thing was too minor to be such a big issue. Bill had made the mistake of disagreeing with Fent in a political discussion, and he was not able to see when he had gone too far and had raised Fent's seldom-invoked temper. They had exchanged heated words, and Fent had suspended their relationship since then. To Fent, Bill was a youngster who had not yet learned how to be circumspect. He often seemed much younger than Nick, even though he was twenty-three.

With a small sigh, Fent said, "Yes, my dear. I remember."

"Anyway," said Nick, recovering the mood, "you know they've brought back presents, Fent. Let's go!"

"All right," agreed Fent, thinking that this was as good a time as any to make peace. "Would you like to go, Luty?"

"No, Fent. I still have some things to do here. Mother and the girls and I will call on them later. You two go on. Give them my best."

"'Bye," said Nick hurriedly, holding the door open for Noland.

Nick jumped down the steps to the ground, then leaped between the gateposts and down the stone steps to the dusty street. He turned and waited for Noland. "I've never been to St. Louis. I'll bet they had a good time," he said. "What do you think they brought me, Fent?"

Fent laughed, despite the fact that he was trying act like the solemn elder brother. "Why, Nick, I'll bet they never even gave you a thought. It was their honeymoon, after all." He could see that Nick gave that notion no credence at all.

"Was your father excited when you left the house?" asked Noland to ease into what he really wanted to find out.

"He tried to pretend he wasn't, but he was. You know how he is about the girls." They walked in silence for a few moments. Then, "Fent, did Father really spit on Mr. Estabrook yesterday?"

"Yes. Well, he spat *at* him, but I don't think it reached him."

"Phil said that somebody told him that Father pulled his nose, too."

"Really. The rumors grow, don't they? Well, I didn't see that happen, but you know your Father. He gets pretty angry. He might have done it. But I don't think so. What did Phil think about it?"

"Oh, he always takes up for Father. But I think he's not as sure about yesterday as he usually is. Why would Father attack a minister? Nobody pays any attention to the kind of remark Mr. Estabrook made at the camp meeting. It's not like last year, because I think Mr. Carter really was saying bad things about Father."

Noland was silent for a moment as he tried to estimate how much Nick knew about his father's financial difficulties back in Holly Springs. He decided to steer away from anything that Nick might interpret as support of Carter's comments, and therefore an attack on Burton. But Nick needed to know his father was not a saint.

"I'm glad to hear you say that, Nick. It's no disrespect to your father to say that he sometimes goes too far. You're old enough to make your own decisions about that. And you'll have to decide how you will handle insults, somewhere along the line. If you allow yourself to be too easily offended by what other people do, you'll get pulled into defending your honor again and again. And once you start down that path, somebody's going to get hurt. Or killed." He lapsed into silence, but Nick knew he was thinking about his own duel, when he had killed the governor's nephew.

By that time, they were across the street from the imposing brick neo-classical State Bank building. In 1837, even before the main State Bank in Little Rock had opened, the Batesville branch had elected a board that had selected Egner's grocery on Main Street as the temporary place of business, which opened in January of 1838. It had also approved the construction of an impressive new building, a two-story Greek revival building with four Doric columns, located on the northwest corner of Main and Spring. The $15,000 structure was probably the most expensive building in north Arkansas, and certainly the most impressive in Batesville. The young bank ran short of capital before it was finished, and the board had had to borrow money from three of the citizens, Trent C. Aiken, Jesse Bean, and John Ruddell. But there it stood, in all its surprising Greek glory, right there on Main Street.

Fent looked across Spring Street at the Day, Williams benches and waved at the two men sitting there in the sun. They turned the corner and passed the benches alongside the McGuire store. They were filled, but when the men spotted Nick walking with Fent, the conversation stopped. In the sudden silence, several men waved a finger at them, and there was a chorus of "Afternoon, Fent" and "Hi, Nick" from the crowd. Both Nick and Fent knew they had been rehashing the excitement of the day before. The two waved and walked on without stopping.

At the next corner, they turned to the left and walked up South Street past Joe Egner's fine two-story house. Egner was an early settler in Batesville who had begun as a clerk for Charles Kelly, but who now had extensive farmland in the bottoms and a mercantile store of his own. He lived one block south of Main Street. He and Noland were good friends. Noland had sadly reported Egner's death in a steamboat sinking in 1837. Noland's note on his death was published in the *Spirit of the Times*, only to be followed a week later by his joyful announcement that Egner had been saved.

Up ahead William Byers's house was on the left, and the Burton house was on the right.Dr. Burton was renting his house while he built his own. It had originally been built for his brother by Townsend Dickinson, who was elected a state representative when Arkansas became a state in 1836. When he was then made one of the supreme court justices, Noland had taken his place in the General Assembly. Dickinson moved permanently to Little Rock, providing for his brother in Batesville by helping him purchase the house. They had been forced to move, however, leaving the house available for the Burtons to rent. The house was adequate for a small family, but the Burtons were finding it a little cramped, which was why Dr. Burton was starting the process of building a new one up the street.

As it happened, the Burton carriage was just driving up to the front of the house as Nick and Fent arrived. Bill Hynson leaped out and helped Rosalie down, then Nannie. The two young women cried "Nick!" and promptly buried him in hugs, to which Nick made no resistance, a sign of his increasing maturity. Bill, beaming, looked at Fent, and his smile froze on his face. Fent looked impassively back at Bill for a moment, then allowed a slight smile to break out on his lips as he took a step forward and extended his hand. Bill seized it and pumped it up and down effusively. The Burton threesome saw the healing gesture, and Rosalie glided up to Fent with a soft, "Oh, Fent," and kissed him on the cheek. Nannie followed suit on the other cheek and, irrepressible as always, burst out, "Well, now that that's over, let's look at all the wonderful presents we have for everyone. Let's go in."

All five bustled up to the front door and went in to greet Dr. Burton, leaving the servants to cope with the impressive pile of baggage. Fent was pleased to see how Nick's face glowed from the excitement of having his sisters back home. He was always delighted to see that Nick was a happy young man...

At his side, Lucretia gave in to a new burst of sobs. When she laid her head on his shoulder, Fent's reverie was shattered and he was forced to return to the tragic reality of Nick's funeral.

8
FAREWELL
TO NICK—III

Friday, October 22, 1841

Giving up on trying to penetrate Noland's unreadable sad
face, Juba Estabrook let his eyes wander toward the rear of the
church. He almost gasped out loud when his eyes fell on Jesse
and Nancy Bean, with Jane Aikin, in a back pew. *What courage!*
he thought, for he, along with everyone else in town, knew
very well that Trent Aiken had already been convicted in the
minds of many of the people in this sanctuary. Dr. Burton had
already posted a $1000 reward for the arrest and return of Aiken,
who had fled into the night. As soon as the sheriff had let the
escape be known, Burton had exploded with rage, convinced
beyond all doubt that Aiken was the man he sought. Sheriff
Engles—yes, there he was, with his family—had been unfairly
criticized by Burton for letting Aiken slip away. Noland also
seemed to be convinced of Aiken's guilt, because he had promised to write and publish a flyer describing the murder and
the murderer for distribution throughout Arkansas in hopes of
getting someone to claim the reward.

Well, Estabrook thought, we need to focus now on grief
and farewell, rather than retribution. But getting this congregation to move to the posture of prayer might prove to be
difficult. He looked over at Mr. Hunt, the Methodist minister

who ran the Batesville Academy where Nick had attended school, sitting on the other side of the low podium, the pulpit between the two of them. The open coffin rested on sawhorses in front of the pulpit, on the congregation's level. Henry Hunt seemed miserable, but he had agreed to offer some words of eulogy. Whatever he said, it would be well received, because he was Nick's teacher and had liked him. Estabrook would have been eager to minister by doing the entire service, but after his infamous encounter with Dr. Burton, he felt certain that his preaching would be unacceptable, and he had not even tried to raise the question with the Burtons. He had asked Hunt to serve, and Hunt had agreed, but reluctantly. There were other Methodist ministers who could have been pressed into service, but Hunt knew Nick from school. Two ministers would be enough. For his part, Estabrook was not willing to relinquish the entire service, because he was the minister of this Methodist church, and Dr. Burton would just have to hear the Scripture and prayers come from his mouth, like it or not.

Judging that it was time to begin and recalling that Dr. Burton had requested a brief service, he stepped to the pulpit and welcomed the congregation here on this sad occasion. He told them that the ladies of the town had provided refreshments that would be served on the church lawn afterward, but that the Burtons had requested that only family come to the house afterward. Estabrook then invited them to open their hearts to the healing of Christ. He read the familiar biblical passages with great feeling, and he felt that the words were having some effect on the mourners. He invited them to pray with him, With practiced voice and biblical phrases he lifted their hearts, showed them the love and mercy of God, and brought them back to this world in hope. He sat and mopped his brow.

Henry Hunt stood and went slowly to the pulpit. Holding his handkerchief in his hand, he began. "Many of us here today have loved Nicholas Burton—some of you all his life,"—he looked at the Burtons—"some of us for only a year. I taught him, and I found it easy to love a boy who liked learning, who had a cheerful spirit, who made all those around him feel better because he was there, who was both graceful and gracious. Now he is gone from us." He paused, and everyone could see the effort he had to make to maintain control.

"We cannot say why. We cannot understand why. But he is gone, and we are diminished.

"His life offered much promise. We all hoped for a naval career for him. Some dared hope for great things when he came to his full maturity. All of us anticipated a full harvest in his adult life of those excellent qualities that we had already recognized in his youth. But God in His wisdom has seen fit to take him to be with Him." He made the mistake of looking down at the pale face of Nick in the coffin below him, and it was almost his undoing. He choked, and had to mop his eyes with his handkerchief.

"What can I say?" he asked in a quivering voice. "We loved him, and will always love him. But he is now in the hands of God, who loves him—nay, has always loved him—eternally." He choked up again, and after a moment he seemed to be trying to say more, but he gave it up. He stumbled to his seat and sat looking down at his lap. In the silence Estabrook became aware of the sounds of grief that filled the church. Estabrook looked out upon a sea of women given over to sobbing, with some of the men dabbing at their eyes with handkerchiefs.

How am I going to turn this into an occasion of joy? wondered Estabrook. Wisely, he concluded that was beyond his ability. He stood and motioned for the stewards to bring the Burtons up for their last look. They came heavily, with Nannie almost carried by Phil, who looked as if he needed help himself. Rosalie leaned on Bill. Dr. Burton, who was dry-eyed and stiff, came alone. The congregation could not look away as each of the Burtons said his or her last emotional goodbye to Nick, then was led back to the pew to await the preparation of the coffin.

When they were finished, Estabrook asked the congregation to stand and sing "Amazing Grace." As the familiar hymn began, two pallbearers quietly brought the coffin lid into place and quickly screwed it down. The other pallbearers stepped up, and they lifted the coffin to their shoulders. They marched carefully down the aisle and down the few steps to the street. The public graveyard was diagonally across the street intersection. The huge crowd outside rolled back and allowed the coffin through. In just a few moments the coffin was in place beside the open grave. The straps were passed under, and the pallbearers gently lowered the wooden box into the hole.

Juba Estabrook arrived, accompanied by a more composed Henry Hunt. They were followed by the Burtons and hundreds of mourners. The Beans' quiet departure after they emerged from the church was noted by many. The rest of the people stood craning to look into the grave or at the Burtons as Estabrook offered one more scripture reading, this one from St. Paul on the resurrection, and offered a final prayer. Each of the Burtons, and many of the mourners, then took turns tossing a bit of dirt on the coffin. Several of them winced at the hollow sound, but all those close to Nick forced themselves to do it as their recognition of the finality of his death. The service was over, and the congregation began to disperse, leaving the filling of the grave to the workers after they had departed.

The Burtons moved slowly down toward their house in a tight stricken cluster. Everyone within a block distinctly heard the words that unexpectedly came from Dr. Burton's hoarse throat: "God damn the man!" Everyone who heard knew that he had uttered neither profanity, nor coarseness, but an Old Testament curse in which the vengeance of God—and Dr. P. P. Burton—had been invoked.

9
THE INQUEST

Saturday, October 23, 1841

The brick courthouse in the Public Square was packed. It was Saturday, a day when many people normally made their trips from the farm to town to purchase supplies and catch up on the community news. This Saturday had the added attraction of the inquest. Gossip about the killing had flown through the county, but nothing official had yet been said. The inquest would provide the first authoritative information about the murder, and the meeting was open to the public. Only a hanging could have provided more excitement.

The coroner's jury had been selected by lot after the funeral the afternoon before, and those chosen had been quickly notified by runners. Among the fourteen men were Joe Pentecost, John Ringgold, and Bobby Bates, owner of the tavern and inn across the street from the Ringgold home. Each of the fourteen would receive $2.25 for his service to the county.

When Joe Egner arrived, he managed to squeeze himself into the rear of the courthouse, where he stood leaning against the wall. It wasn't a bad position for him, he realized. He could see all over the courtroom, and he didn't mind standing for the short gathering. He couldn't see the faces of the people on the benches, but he had no trouble recognizing them. Henry Engles, of course, had a much better position. He sat at a clerk's table in the front corner of the room, where he had paper and pen ready to take his own notes as the testimony was given. He would receive the official record of the meeting, but he apparently expected to have his own observations that needed to be noted for further action.

Egner spotted John and Clara Miller and their eighteen-year-old son Bill sitting on the rear bench with Jesse and Nancy Bean and Jane Aiken. The Aikens's children were not present, which Egner thought a good decision. He looked around the room and saw all of the families closely affected by the death of Nick Burton. Without running a count, he also noted that there was a good showing of people who were friends and supporters of Aiken and his extended family.

Egner was clear in his own mind that Aiken was not responsible for the boy's death. The man was a doctor, a man to be trusted. Moreover, he was a family man and, as far as Egner had ever been able to see, a good man. Aiken was one of the leading figures in the Democratic party here in Independence County, and it had not escaped Egner that all of the aggrieved families in the case were Whigs. It would be wise, he thought, to keep politics to a minimum in this situation and try to keep everyone focused on justice.

He was a realist, however, and he knew that people automatically tended to believe the best of the people most like them, while they were all too often ready to believe the worst of those who were different. No, he reflected, it would be wise for Henry Engles to use his authority to keep everyone in order until the murderer was caught, because the mood of the people called for a swift resolution of the case, and justice could easily be lost in the process.

Would the killer be caught, though? Engles was as good a sheriff as was normally needed in Independence County, but this murder was far beyond the usual problem. How would he find the assassin? Did he know enough? Would he be strong enough to protect Trent Aiken? Egner had to admit to himself that he didn't know the answers to his questions.

The noise in the courtroom was loud, as everyone there had something to talk about with his neighbor. What made it even harder was the scuffling of shoes over the rough brick floor as people fidgeted in anticipation. People were still squeezing into the small courtroom, and many of them, Egner noted, made it a point to stop at the rear bench and speak to John Miller and Jesse Bean. Both Miller and Bean were in their fifties, and they were both widely respected throughout the county. Both were early settlers in the county, both were leaders in the Democratic party, and both had military titles. Colonel Miller had been born in Virginia, but the Millers had been in Arkansas since 1814. Miller's rank as colonel was like that of so many men throughout the nation—he had been elected colonel of the local militia by the men, a post that he filled for years, but he had not seen major military action. It was an honor to be so trusted by the citizen-soldiers, though, and most colonels bore the title to their graves. Miller's popularity in the county was reflected in his having been elected twice in state politics as a Democratic party elector.

With Jesse Bean, it was another story. Jesse's rank as captain was earned, because he had years of experience in the regular army. He had raised his company of mounted riflemen with young men primarily from Independence County, and they had spent most of the years of 1832 and 1833 together enjoying the hard life of nomadic hunters on the plains to the west. The exploits of "Bean's Rangers" were still talked about in the county, even though they had never seen military action, because they had had well publicized adventures, thanks to Mr. Irving's book about the experience. Egner silently noted the presence of many of those Rangers in the courthouse. There were still twenty-five or so who still lived in the county and bore their identity proudly. And, Egner knew, they were always pleased to speak to "Cap'n Bean" when they crossed his path. They would be a good source of help if trouble came over the Burton killing, Egner reflected, and made a mental note to mention it to Henry Engles.

With a bang of the gavel John Miniken brought the room to silence. His job as temporary coroner, appointed by the sheriff and the bed-ridden coroner, was to determine whether

deaths were to be referred to the sheriff and the courts for
legal action. Miniken was nervous, because he was out of his
element. Rarely were the county coroners called upon to deal
with a case as fraught with legal problems as this one was
likely to be. The mysterious death of Nick Burton was a rare
occurrence.

Miniken had eschewed the judge's bench to emphasize
that this was not a court. He sat at a table in front, flanked
by young Jasper Blackburn, who worked at the *Batesville
News* and was already considered a competent writer. Mort
Baltimore, the coroner, had "volunteered" him to keep the
minutes of the meeting, so Blackburn was equipped with
paper, pens, and ink. With no one in the jail, it was already
clear that the decision of the coroner could be no stronger
than a vague conclusion that murder had been done, but the
notes of the testimony and the names of the witnesses might
prove to be of use to the sheriff as the case moved toward pros-
ecution. In any case, there had to be a legal record.

The first witnesses were quickly finished. Rutherford
Herriott, a local farmer, told of passing Nick on the road north
of Miller Creek that morning, and Ben Wilson outlined Nick's
visit to his house and their conversation about the shingles.
The large audience became intensely silent as Boney Allen
told his story. Then Henry Bales, one of the men who had
gone to the death scene, told of the discovery of the body and
the search for clues. Ringgold would have given that testimony, but he was on the coroner's jury, so he was not called.
Most of the testimony was already known to Miller, who had
been filled in by Bean on what his slaves knew. When Miller
was called, it was just for the purpose of ascertaining that he
knew nothing about the case, except for the presence of Jesse
Bean in his house during the crucial time.

There was a stir in the courtroom when Dr. Burton was
called. The crowd became silent and watched the solemn handsome face as Burton walked to the witness chair and sat. The
sheriff had offered to have Dr. Chapman examine Nick's body,
but Dr. Burton had insisted it was his job—and his son—so the

sheriff had backed off. Dr. Chapman had "assisted" Burton at the brief final examination. There was no autopsy, since both doctors agreed there was no need. Burton told the court that there were eleven buckshot in the back of the head and upper back, and that they had penetrated far enough to cause instant death but not far enough to emerge on the other side of the body. He estimated that the shotgun had been fired from somewhere behind the victim at a distance of thirty to fifty yards. Dr. Burton was able to complete his testimony with no break in his professional composure; everyone noted that he was almost cold in his delivery. That was a disappointment for those who wanted fireworks, but most were relieved that the doctor's temper was not in evidence. Then Sheriff Engles spoke briefly, largely just confirming the testimony that had been given.

There was another stir when Miniken called Bean's young slave Richard to the front, an irregular procedure, but everyone listened intently as he described Aiken's movements on Thursday. Under Miniken's questioning he added a detail he had not told the sheriff, that he did not see or hear anyone passing on the road in either direction in the time between the sound of the shotgun and Dr. Aiken's return to the house. To a question from the sheriff, though, he admitted he could not swear that no one could have passed by unseen. Jesse Bean was called for his testimony, but he could add nothing to the story, other than to attest to the trustworthiness of his slaves and to say his son-in-law was out of town, location unknown. That statement, anticipated though it was, brought an uproar of conversation in the room that lasted for a few minutes, until Miniken's pounding on the table finally brought silence.

Egner could see on the faces of many people that Aiken's absence was already known and discussed. He also sensed from the covert looks at Miller and the Beans that many believed that Aiken had done the killing. The case against him looked even stronger when another witness—a surprise to Egner—was called forward. David Tinkey testified that he had been returning from a business journey up the bayou road in the late morning and had passed Aiken on his horse heading up the road. When he had reached the path into the Bean household he had seen Richard and had stopped and asked him where Dr. Aiken had been going in such a hurry, thinking it was a medical emergency. The boy had told him that Dr. Aiken had gone "after Nick Burton." Miniken called no more witnesses and the jury conferred five minutes before ruling, as expected, that Nick Burton had died of gunshot wounds by person or persons unknown. He banged the gavel and allowed the people—and the town—to return to excited conversation.

Fent Noland was not called to testify, so Egner had no chance to assess his emotional state. Nor could he see his face, which he regretted, because there was always the chance that Fent would betray his thoughts in reaction to what he heard. He resolved to make it a point to speak to Noland briefly before he vanished to his day's activities, to try to get a time for Egner to visit with him. Perhaps Henry would like to go with him. He could think of several good reasons for talking with Ringgold and Noland about the whole affair, among them the close connection of Fent with the Burtons.

John Miller rose and ushered his family and the Beans out of the courthouse, feeling the quizzical stares of the people who stepped aside to let them through. Egner watched them go, then began to work his way forward to talk with Henry Engles.

10

A VISIT WITH FENT

Monday, October 25, 1841

Joe Egner walked down South Street alongside Henry, who led his horse by the reins. Engles had ridden to Egner's house from Engleside, then the two of them were continuing on to the Ringgold house. Egner saw no reason to saddle a horse for the brief trip, so the two of them walked together. In an effort to reduce public gossip about their movements, they were taking the back street to Block 10, where the Ringgold house and farmstead occupied the whole block. They intended to slip into the house by the back door, as unnoticed as possible.

Even from the back yard the Ringgold house was attractive. It was a wide brick house that looked as if it had been imported from Maryland, Ringgold's original home. The dormers on the roof betrayed a second floor where additional bedrooms were reached by an interior stairway in the central hall. The two attached rooms on the ends of the house served as parlor and office. Noland had taken over the office as his own even before his marriage to Lucretia, for he had lived there with the Ringgolds for years after his return from his military tour.

When the two men entered the rear gate, they found a man hoeing around the still-producing vegetable plants in the garden. The man dropped the hoe and came over to take the sheriff's horse.

"Morning, gentlemen," said the middle-aged slave.

"Mister Fent said you would be calling. Front door or back door?"

"We'll just go in the back, Ed," said Engels.

"Show these gentlemen in to see Mister Fent, Mary," Ed said to the smiling young girl who had come from the kitchen, dispatched by the cook.

"Yes, papa," she said gravely, then with dignity she led them to the back door and held it for them. Inside the hallway, she ran quickly to the parlor door, stuck her head in the opening, and said, "Mister Fent, your company's here." She stood back as Noland stepped into the hall, hand extended. He was in shirt sleeves, but fully dressed for the day, except for his scarf. Egner noted that his face looked drawn, and he seemed even more frail than usual. With Fent, though, it was always hard to tell when he was not doing well, because his consumption flared up frequently, and his weight varied from slender to thin. At thirty-one, he looked young and neat, but not quite healthy.

"Come in, Joe, Henry," he said as he shook their hands. They went into the parlor and took seats. After they refused the offer of something to drink, Noland said, "John had some things to tend to at the store, so he said if you want to talk with him, just send a servant for him and he will come over." Ringgold's two-story brick mercantile store, where he kept his office, was across the street and up one block, convenient for Ringgold to visit off and on through the day.

"Thanks, Fent," said Henry. "I'm not sure John can tell us anything you can't. We'll see. We just really wanted to talk with you about the tragedy. You've got a better handle on this than most people, I guess, because you were so close to Nick. I'd like to know how you've put all this together in your mind."

Fent looked at him for a moment, then said, "I can't make it fit together very well. It's hard to believe that Nick is dead..." He sighed and paused for a moment. He looked at Egner and said, "It's as hard as when you were dead, Joe." Egner's thin smile was all the affectionate response he could muster. All three of the men recalled well the time four years earlier when Egner had been reported lost in the Mississippi River in a steamboat explosion. He saved himself by floating downstream on a log, but it took additional days for the news of his survival to reach Batesville.

"But Nick won't be coming back," Noland sighed. "You know, it's even harder to believe that someone killed him. I keep trying to come up with some reason. Did Nick have any enemies? Nobody thinks so. I asked Mr. Hunt, and he knows of no one at school who had any problem with Nick. I asked Phil if Nick had any relationship with a girl." He looked at them and shrugged. "Lots of strange things can happen when love and jealousy are part of the story. But Phil says 'no,' and he would know, I think."

"What does Dr. Burton think?" asked Joe Egner.

"I asked him. He doesn't have any notion beyond Trent Aiken. He's sure Aiken shot him."

"Why does he think that? I know he despises Trent, but that's not enough to convict a man of murder," Engles pointed out.

"Well, there's the place, for one thing. You have to believe strongly in coincidence to ignore the fact that Nick was shot after passing by Aiken's place. And then Aiken immediately fled the county. Dr. Burton doesn't need any more than that."

"And you?" Engles asked.

"And me. I'd be happy to learn that Trent didn't do it, but I don't think that's much of a possibility. Why would he run? Where is he? Why didn't he leave a letter or send one from wherever he is? That looks like the act of a guilty man to me."

"I understand that argument, Fent," Joe said. "It's pretty powerful. But I have a hard time seeing Aiken doing something like that. Maybe in an argument, maybe in the heat of a dispute. But just to go out to the road and shoot Nick in the back? They were friends, weren't they? I don't know. Seems wrong."

"Do any of us really know him, though? Did you know before he and Dr. Burton got into their fight that he was a coward? I didn't. I would never have said beforehand that he would refuse a challenge, but he did. I lost my respect for him when he did that. How could he hold his head up around here? I think that finished him. First Burton called his medical competence into question, then he tested his honor. And Trent failed."

"Fent," Henry said softly. "I mean no disrespect, but I have to say this. Not everybody sees the dispute and the challenge the way you do. You responded to a challenge when it came to you, and you showed your courage, and Pope died. So you can take a strong position on challenges. You have nothing to prove. From my viewpoint as sheriff, though, dueling is against the law, and it ought to be. I respect Buck Woodruff's refusal to answer a challenge a while back." He was referring to the *Arkansas Gazette* editor's standing policy of refusing invitations to duels. "We'd have a lot of dead editors if they accepted challenges. Or editors who don't say much. I think it takes a lot of courage to refuse a duel, and I'm not alone in feeling that way."

Fent sighed. "You may be right, Henry. I'll admit I'm sorry about my duel. It may be time for dueling to stop. My father believes that strongly. He was very angry with me about mine." Noland leaned forward earnestly. "But I'll wager most people in this county don't take that view. Do you think Aiken refused to fight on principle?"

"I don't know, Fent," Engles replied. "I've never talked with him about it, but I wouldn't be surprised. What would have happened if you had refused to fight Fontaine Pope?"

"I think I would have been ruined in Arkansas. Just like Aiken is, regardless of why he refused the challenge. I'll bet most people around here think Aiken is a coward. You know what that means. He should have stood up to Dr. Burton."

"Standing up to Dr. Burton when he's got his dander up would take a lot for most people," Egner said with a slight frown. "Maybe we ought to respect Aiken for refusing. Would you really want to deal with Burton when he's in one of his rages?"

"Well, no. I wouldn't," Fent admitted. "But that's what courage is about. Sometimes you just get backed into a corner, and you have to do something you don't want to do."

"I'd like to raise a slightly different question, if that's all right," said Henry. The others looked at him expectantly. "It's this business of killing a son of somebody you're mad at. It seems to make sense to Dr. Burton that Aiken would shoot Nick to get back at him. Does that make sense to you, Fent?"

"Not any ordinary kind of sense. But I think it is possible for some people to go crazy and start thinking in a different way. Our normal kind of sense isn't theirs. You know that's true—crazy people will do anything. Just like a mad dog. And when a madman kills somebody, even strangers, you know it must make some kind of sense to him. Who knows what his dispute with Burton has done to Aiken? Maybe killing Nick got to where it seemed right to him. What do you think, Joe? Has Aiken gone crazy?"

"If he has, Fent, it has happened since I saw him two weeks ago. I wish I had had a chance to talk with him about Dr. Burton. It's been two weeks since I've even seen Trent, but I didn't see any signs of anything more than worry over his troubles with Burton. Same as any of us would have experienced." Egner paused a moment, looking distantly through the front window onto Main Street. "I don't guess I know what a killer madman looks like, Fent. I was telling Henry that I have less trouble imagining Burton as one than Aiken."

"What!" Fent burst out. "What are you saying? That Burton killed his own son?"

"No, no, no. I don't believe that at all. I'm just saying that—well, when you say 'crazy,' the first person I think of is P. P. Burton. You know what I'm talking about. Juba Estabrook ran afoul of him, and he got a public attack from Burton, right here on Main Street. And how about Burton's fight with Tom Carter? He took a stick to him, right up there at Spit Corner.

And why? Just because he had *heard* Carter was gossiping about him. Carter was ready to get a gun and go after him, he was so upset. And you know what a calm man Carter is."

Fent leaned back in his chair, studying his shoes. "I see. I can't say that I haven't thought about that, Joe, because I have. Burton's got a very bad temper, and he doesn't seem to have much control over it. I've worried over how to help Nick think about that unpleasant aspect of his father, but I never got very far with it. But crazy? I never thought of it that way before. I've seen bad tempers, and Burton's is just a little worse than the ones I've seen. I'm not sure that's crazy, but it is a flaw. Most definitely a flaw."

"Maybe so, Fent, but it's a flaw that scares people, I think. I'll wager you will find that most people are real nervous about Burton. They watch what they say around him. They are –what do I want to say?–*wary* of him. Flawed or crazy, people avoid him. He's like a powder keg, and you don't know what the fuse is."

"That may be so, Joe, but it doesn't affect the important fact here. Burton did not kill his son. You may be right that he is a little touched, but the most you could say about that is that he has the ability to make other people scared of him. You said Tom Carter was about to get a gun. Think about that. You were saying that Burton made even Carter become violent. Maybe that's just a step away from making people crazy. Like Aiken?"

"But if that's so, Fent, then maybe Carter or Estabrook is the killer. Have you thought about that?" Egner asked. Noland looked at him quizzically and slowly raised one eyebrow.

With a deep breath, Engles shook his head and said, "This has been a helpful conversation, Fent. I've got to get on, though. I've got lots to do today. Thanks for helping me think about all this. Joe, you coming, or do you want to stay and visit?" Henry rose and extended his hand to Noland.

"I need to go along, too," Egner said as he stood. "I'll be talking to you again, Fent. We've got a lot to think through before all this is done."

"One thing is clear, I think," said Fent. "Aiken needs to get himself back here. Without him, he sure looks like the killer. It might look the same if he were here, but we can't know that, can we?"

"No," Engles responded. "You're right about that, Fent. We need Aiken to come home."

"You know about the Young Men's meeting tomorrow evening?" Noland asked as he escorted them to the back door down the hall.

"I heard something about it," said the sheriff. "What on the program? Buying a grave marker, I heard. Anything else?"

"Just speeches and talk, I think. We need a forum to discuss all this. You need to come, Henry. Listen to what people are saying about Nick's murder."

As the two visitors walked down South Street toward the Courthouse, Egner said, "That was abrupt. There was more to be said, I thought."

The sheriff turned toward Egner and said, "Well, I kind of thought the conversation had gone far enough. I didn't want it to look like I was taking sides. It seems to me that we accomplished one thing this morning. We gave Fent a good rationale for the murder: Burton can make anyone crazy enough to want to kill."

After a silent moment, Egner turned to Engles and said, "You know what worries me, Henry? I'm not sure the killing's over." Henry's eyes widened as Joe's comment sank in.

11

A CIVIC MEETING

Tuesday, October 26, 1841

Noland did not have to go far to get to his meeting the next night. The "Young Men" were meeting right across Main Street from the Ringgold house. Since there really was no public hall for meetings in Batesville, any gathering had to take place at either the Methodist Church, the courthouse, or whatever tavern was available at the time. For tonight's gathering the Batesville Hotel had been selected. A posted notice told anyone who merely wanted to go to a tavern that he had to choose whether to attend the meeting or find another place to drink.

This inn had been built almost twenty years before by Robert Bates, an Irishman who had come to town from the east coast at the same time Batesville was being born. He had done well in the tavern business, and people across Arkansas who had done business in Batesville knew him. Bates was not the current proprietor, but some of the locals still liked to joke that the town had been named for him.

Everyone in the Batesville area seemed to be here, and the place was packed already. There was a high level of outrage about the murder in the community, and this meeting would provide one means of expression of that outrage. The Young Men's Meeting was an institution in Batesville. It was unorganized in the sense that there was no membership roll, no dues, and no regular time for meetings. When there was a reason for gathering, and sometimes when there wasn't, the unofficial leaders—the Whig leaders who had state-level connections, like Ringgold, Noland, and several plantation owners out in the county—would call a meeting, and it would happen. It was modeled on the political party meetings, and this one probably began as a Whig Young Men's gathering, but if so, it had long since lost any partisan identity. It served too many useful purposes in Batesville for it to be restricted to politics, particularly politics of one persuasion. Issues of the day got discussed here, community spirit was expressed here, lectures for edification were given here. The "young men" were actually men of any age who wished to attend, so the gathering served as a town business meeting, even though there were usually no women present.

Joe Egner sat with Henry Engles against a wall where they could see everyone. They saw with satisfaction that the meeting was well attended. When Fent came into the room, they watched to see where he would sit. P. P. and Phil Burton were sitting quietly at a table in the corner with the Hynson boys. They spotted John Miller and Jesse Bean across the room surrounded by some of the Rangers from years past.

Noland shook hands with several people as he came in, and he waved at several more. He turned down two offers of a drink. He leaned against a wall close to the front, seemingly content to have no seat.

There was a ringing of metal on glass, and the raucous conversation began to die away as expectant looks were directed at Mark Reinhardt, one of the many fine lawyers in Batesville. "Gentlemen," he said loudly, "let me begin our gathering by moving that William Davis be elected to the chair, and that Mr. Shaw and Mr. Alexander be elected secretaries." There was a roar of approval, underscored by the thump of many glasses on wooden tabletops. "Anyone in disagreement?" Reinhardt asked. Silence. Everyone knew this was all pre-arranged.

Davis rose and went to the table by the wall amid scattered applause. Shaw and Alexander took seats close by him and laid their already prepared writing materials on the table in front of them. Davis immediately announced that unless there were objections, he would call upon Fent Noland to explain the purpose of the night's meeting. There was a chorus of approval, and Noland stepped up alongside Davis. He briefly pointed out that all minds were on the murder of Nick Burton, and that this gathering had been called to determine ways in which respect for the deceased could be demonstrated, perhaps some sort of memorial, and surely a written resolution that could be published. He returned to his spot against the wall. Davis, sensing unanimous agreement in the group, suggested that he be granted permission to appoint a committee to draft a resolution. Everyone knew the procedure quite well, because it was the way in which the Masonic order, Batesville's political meetings, and the previous Young Men's meetings had all been conducted, so there was immediate applause for him to do it. He thereupon appointed to the resolutions committee C. F. M. Noland, J. C. Knettle, J. L. Fraley, James McGibbeny, and Jesse Searcy. Davis sent them out to do their work. As they left, many spotted the rolled up paper in Noland's hand and knew that the deliberations would not take long. Noland was, after all, the town's celebrated writer, and he had obviously already done his job.

While the committee retired to an unused room in the hotel, the main group began to discuss ways that proper respect could be shown for the murdered youth. After an animated discussion that at times threatened to branch off into theories about the murder, Davis called for motions. By that time it was clear that the motion for all men to wear black armbands in Batesville for a month in Nick's honor would be acceptable without further discussion, and that proved to be the case.

A motion to raise a fund to purchase a special stone monument to mark Nick's grave was more troublesome. There were comments that the grave belonged to the family, but that argument was countered by the suggestion that the monument would need to receive the full approval of the family before they went any further with it. Dr. Burton nodded without comment. One man asked whether a stone monument was not an unwarranted expenditure by the townspeople, but a hasty whispered conference at his table made it clear to him that there would be ample money donated, and that if Dr. Burton could offer a $1000 reward, he could certainly be counted on to make up any shortfall. He withdrew his question, and the motion was approved unanimously.

Davis appointed another committee of five to carry the work forward by creating a design, collecting the money, and arranging with the stonemasons for the construction of the monument. Mark Reinhardt was named chair, and he immediately suggested that, since the resolutions committee had not yet returned, the gathering carry on a discussion of the style of the monument for the edification of the committee. Davis invited comments, and in just a few minutes the group had arrived at some sort of an unusual design, one not normally found on graves. One of those with military experience suggested a catafalque, a tablet resting on four upturned cannon. The objection that Nick was not yet a military man, even though he might have become a naval officer, resulted in the compromise to transform the cannon into vertical columns supporting a rectangular tablet with no decoration beyond the engraved name, "Nicholas E. Burton." Those ideas were then turned over to the committee.

At that point the resolutions committee returned. It had taken longer than expected, most learned later, because Noland's previously written resolution named Trent C. Aiken as the murderer, and several of the committee had pointed out to him that there were many men in the gathering, including themselves, who were not as convinced as Noland was that Aiken was the killer. They argued that, whether or not Noland proved to be right, the inclusion of the name would lead to a heated debate in the meeting and might result in the failure to pass the resolution, which would be something of a disgrace. Noland yielded and struck the name. He did not reveal that he had already sent off a note from "N. of Arkansas" to the *Spirit of the Times* in New York in which he mentioned the murder and identified the killer as "a base, cowardly wretch, named Trent C. Akin, (by profession a doctor)." He also did not tell them that the *Batesville News* coming out Thursday would also carry his editorial naming Aiken.

At Davis's request, Noland read the resolution:

"WHEREAS—On the evening of the 21st inst., a most atrocious and cold blooded murder was perpetrated upon the person of our esteemed young friend and fellow townsman, Nicholas E. Burton, under circumstances so at war with every thing belonging to Christianity, and so unattended with any mitigating causes, that independent of the deep hold on our affections, which our young friend's boldness of character, kindness of heart, and frankness of manner has won, we should be wanting in our duty, as good citizens, not to make our public disapproval of this most foul and unnatural murder. In order to do so, therefore, and to pay that tribute to the memory of our young friend which his thousand bright virtues ably deserve, be it

"*Resolved*, That we sincerely and deeply mourn the loss of our young friend, Nicholas E. Burton, and tender most respectfully to his bereaved parent and relatives, our sympathies, for the heart-rending affections into which this most horrible assassination has plunged them; That we will cause to be erected to his memory a suitable monument, and wear crape on our left arm for the space of thirty days; That we will use our best exertions to wipe from our country the foul stain cast upon it, by bringing to speedy justice, the *cruel, heartless, cowardly* wretch who perpetrated this act—a fiend in human shape, for,

"'Not in the regions
Of horrid hell, can come a devil, more damned
In evils, to top him.'"

The resolution was unanimously and raucously adopted. They quickly voted to have the minutes, with resolution, published in the upcoming issue of the *Batesville News*. With that, Davis adjourned the meeting, and the gathering splintered into noisy discussions of the murder and the missing murderer, and whether Aiken was indeed the guilty one.

12
ANNA'S SECOND
LETTER HOME

Thursday, October 28, 1841

There was a chill in the air during the nights now, and Anna Hynson could not help but feel it was appropriate, considering the chill that had settled over the town in the last week. Only one week, but it seemed like years. Nothing was the same since Nick had been shot. Grief hung over the Burton household, and people in the extended family all walked and talked as if they were carrying a heavy burden. The townspeople, even people who had hardly known Nick, talked of little else, and the speculation as to the whereabouts of Dr. Aiken was endless. He had been spotted in Fayetteville, and was probably in Indian country. He had been seen in Mississippi. He was in disguise in Little Rock. Only one thing was certain— he wasn't in Independence County.

Dr. Burton was a sad case, a man in paralysis. It was as if the only thing in his life that had meaning to him was revenge on Dr. Aiken. He rarely spoke, and when he did it was about avenging Nick's death. There were frequent reports from the many people who were out searching for Aiken, all negative. With $1,000 as a goal, a princely sum, there were many people willing to lose time and suffer inconvenience to go out on the hunt, but no one had been able to claim the prize yet. Phil Burton and Bill Hynson had also been out on overnight jaunts, not for the money, but because they both seemed driven by the same passion for vengeance that dominated Dr. Burton.

There was also a growing chill in relations between people. Anna had been surprised to discover that not everyone was as convinced as the members of her family that Dr. Aiken was the killer. In fact, she had learned, there were a great many people who even thought there was a major injustice in process. She found that very confusing, because if Fent Noland, a reasonable, open-minded man, was convinced that Aiken was the killer, then why did they not see that Aiken was guilty? After all, the testimony at the inquest had left little room for another suspect. Yet there were many people who were very forthright in saying that the sheriff needed to be continuing his investigation, looking for the real murderer.

Tonight the chill had reached Nat, and he had told Anna at the supper table that he wanted to hear no more about the whole thing. That was when she had suggested they work together on letters back home to Maryland to fill them in on what had happened. He had countered by saying he would play with Meddy while she wrote letters, but that he didn't want to talk any more about The Subject.

So here she was, a thoroughly read copy of the *Batesville News* on the chair beside her, paper and pen on the table before her, and no clue as to how to tell people back home about all of this. "Only one way," she thought. "Begin, Anna."

Mrs. McCall Medford
Chestertown, Maryland

> *Batesville, Arks.*
> *October 28, 1841*

My dearest Mother,
> *My last letter to you was written on the 10th of this month. Since then an event has occured which has plunged us all in the deepest affliction. I will endeavor to detail it to you after first informing you that myself and husband continue in excellent health and so had dear Meddy been until lately. He has a*

cold and has been threatened with the croup. I intend
to give him his medicine tomorrow morning and hope
he will soon be restored to his good health. He has his
usually good spirits and is not actually sick.

I shall mail with this letter—I hope it may reach
you at the same time—a publication of Dr. Burton's
giving a description of the difficulty between him
and Dr. Trent which has led to such awful results.
As the paper of Dr. Burton's gives in full the whole
transaction and I expect you to receive it, I do not
deem it necessary to say anything about the difference
except there are persons here who can prove every
fact that Dr. Burton advances. I will proceed to state
what has taken place since the publication. The paper
was issued on Wednesday the 13th and on Thursday
morning Nicholas, Dr. Burton's third son, left home
to procure some shingles for the house Dr. Burton is
building.

Anna re-read what she had written and realized that it
sounded as if Nick had been killed on the 14th. She squeezed
a "(21st)" between the lines, then frowned at the unreadable
mess. "Oh, well," she thought, "I'll send her a copy of the
News with the letter, and that will clarify anything I make
confusing."

Unfortunately he had to pass Doctor Aiken's
residence, about four miles from town. Dr. Aiken
armed himself and repaired to a place in his field
near the road where it was easy to conceal himself,
and awaited poor Nick's return for the purpose of
killing him. As he came on he was accompanied by
a Mr. Allen who says they were talking of partridge
shooting when he heard the report of a gun, turned
his head and saw poor Nick fall dead from his horse.
Allen spurred his horse without looking back to see
who was perpetrator of the deed. He brought the news
to town, and immediately Dr. Burton, Phillip, and

many others repaired to the spot, hoping to find that
he still lived. But, alas, poor youth, his immortal spirit
had departed. Eleven buckshot were found in his back
and the back of his head, poor fellow. It is supposed
he never felt anything. He was killed so instantly that
his whip was found clenched in his hand.

They traced footsteps some distance from the spot
and one of Dr. Burton's publications was found near
there. Not a doubt remained in the mind of many as
to Aiken being a murderer. Dr. Burton wished to go
immediately to his house, but Uncle John persuaded
him not to go. Aiken fled that night and a great
many citizens have been out looking for him but
as yet in vain. Some have not yet returned. They
have heard of him several times. Phillip has gone
with the determination not to return till he finds him.
Dr. Burton says that he will seek him out and avenge
his son's death if it takes him ten years. He has offered
one thousand dollars reward for him. It is generally
thought that Aiken has gone to Texas. Others think
he has gone to Canada.

I do not suppose there was ever such excitement
in any community as there is here.

But was there ever such an unprovoked cold-
blooded assassination before? I never read or heard
of one. Poor Nicholas never harmed Aiken and took
no part in his father's quarrel with Aiken. But if Aiken
had abused Dr. Burton, he would have instantly
resented it, being very quick as well as brave, and
then Aiken would have had the law on his side, but
he was too great a coward to attack a man openly. To
think of his shooting poor Nick in the back without
giving him a moment to resist or prepare for death. It's
truly most awful! The more I think of it the worse it
seems. The family is plunged in distress. Dr. Burton
seems truly miserable and says the only wish he has
on earth is to see Aiken. I have been a great deal at

*Dr. Burton's since the awful event. He always seems
the same. He neither reads nor talks except about the
probability of Aiken's being taken and grasps eagerly
at every account of him. I fear if he could see Aiken
dead it would not ease his mind. But who would
ever have thought of the ... avenging himself on poor
innocent youth! I wish Dr. Burton would allow the
law to take its course, for shooting is too honorable
a death for the murder of poor Nick Burton.*
    The jury decided that Aiken killed him.

"Was "jury" the right word?" she wondered. She had
not attended the inquest herself, and it was not really clear to
her what went on. The *News* article was not very much help
on the details. "Oh, why did Nat refuse to help me? He understands these things. Oh, well."

*Nick was not eighteen, a very handsome young
man of good heart, and very brave. He was awaiting
orders to join the Navy. You will see some account
of the regard which was felt for him in the News
of today, which I send with publication, fearing that
the one which is regularly sent may be lost. I will
call your attention to the obituary notice, also to
the young man's meeting.*

She picked up the *News* and opened it again to the
second page, where the obituary notice was printed. She read
it again, savoring the words. "Mr. Noland has such a gift,"
she thought; "he can catch the mood just right: '...a gloom
hangs over our village and tears are shed by eyes unused to the
melting.' Just right, Fent. Back to the letter, Anna."

*He was buried on Friday with every regard. His
friends had the satisfaction of finding that though his
head was shot, his face was not injured and looked
natural. Reverend Mr. Hunt, to whom he went to
school last winter, made some feeling remarks. He
was much moved in speaking and did not feel himself*

equal to prepare a sermon. I never saw so much
general distress at a funeral. Poor Nick. I can scarcely
believe he is gone. I liked him very much.

When I write again I hope that I will be able to
say that Aiken has been taken, but I much feel that
he will escape entirely. It is thought by some that he
is one of Murrell's band, a most dreadful character
in Tennessee who is now in prison. Aiken came from
that state six years ago. Murrell has been engaged in
negro and horse stealing, and in April last he laid the
plan to rob the branch bank here. But it was supposed
he was prevented by the death of a man on whom he
chiefly depended. He told a man who wished to join
him and the man put the officers of the bank on their
guard, but it was never fully known until now.

"I wonder if that can be true?" she mused. "I never heard
of Murrell before we moved to Arkansas, and I'm sure Mother
has not heard of this at all. Murrell was famous around here,
though." She had learned the story from Eliza in detail over
the last few weeks, and she found it thrilling.

John A. Murrell ran a gang of robbers in west Tennessee and
east Arkansas until his arrest and conviction for slave stealing
in 1834. The major feature of the trial was the testimony of
Virgil A. Stewart, who claimed to have joined Murrell's gang
in order to spy them out and bring them to justice. Stewart
had written some books about the gang. John Ringgold had
told her that it described a huge criminal conspiracy headed
by Murrell. The gang turned into a "Mystic Clan of the
Confederacy" with hundreds of sworn members, many of
whom (named by Stewart), were leaders in their communi-
ties, and even more followers who were simply workers in
the Clan without knowledge of the ultimate plan. That plan
involved creating a huge slave uprising that would topple the
existing order in the lower Mississippi Valley.

Stewart was widely believed, and his revelations had
severe consequences. Eliza Hynson explained to her what
her father had told her: There was a mailing of letters from

northern abolitionists to southern planters, urging them to make their opposition to slavery known. The uproar in the South convinced many that the Stewart books had to be true, and Murrell became in the public mind a crazed abolitionist whose goal was the destruction of Southern society. The Murrell saga became a permanent one. There were a few skeptical arguments raised against Stewart from the beginning, by newspaper editors, in particular, Uncle John said. "Everyone I've heard talk about the Murrell gang seemed convinced it is all true, though, even Eliza," Anna thought.

The Murrell connection with the Burton murder was supported by another story revealing that Murrell and his gang had been planning to rob the State Bank in Batesville. Nat had come in with the story yesterday, something he picked up at the store. "Nick's death had certainly had the effect of producing interesting stories! Who knew about the plan to rob the State Bank? Uncle John? Why didn't he tell anyone before now? Why would he tell the story now? Because the people at the bank think Dr. Aiken was one of the Murrell gang? That seems so unlikely. Could Aiken have fooled them and Captain Bean and Colonel Miller?

"Oh, well. I can't write all this to Mother. She'll be frightened to death. I need to end this letter," she decided abruptly.

> *The murderer, Aiken, has a wife and three*
> *children. Mr. Hynson sends his love and Meddie*
> *is asleep but he thinks much of his grandmother.*
> *Love from your dutiful daughter.*
>
> *Anna M. Hynson*

She laid the pen down on the table and leaned back. She tried to imagine Dr. Aiken as a masked desperado, riding down on a beached flatboat with guns blazing or walking into the State Bank with shotgun at the ready. It was a hard picture to make believable. "But if that was hard to believe, why was it easy to believe that he would shoot Nick in the back?" Disturbed at the direction of her thought, she picked up the *News* again and re-read the article by Noland—it was unsigned, but she was sure he was the author. She glanced through the first part, which just described the event, but read thoughtfully the paragraphs that dealt with the proof that Aiken was the killer:

"Who did the bloody deed, was no sooner asked than answered—all pointed to **Dr. Trent C. Aiken**, as the perpetrator. And why?—The reasons are these:— The murder took place near his house; Dr. Burton and he were engaged in the most bitter controversy, and but a day or two before the murder, had issued a most cutting hand bill against him. The testimony before the inquest showed that Young Burton passed by Aiken's in the morning, and that soon after his passing, Aiken took his gun and put off in the same direction. He met an individual coming down the Bayou—when this individual reached Aiken's gate, a little negro boy came out and asked him if he had met Aiken, and said, "he is after Nick or Dick Burton." It is proved that Aiken returned home, and after getting his dinner, took his gun and proceeded down the road in the direction of the spot where the murder was committed; and that some 30 minutes afterwards, Young Burton passed by on his return. Aiken got back to the house about 20 or 30 minutes after the gun fired. One of Dr. Burton's hand bills was found close to the spot, which, in the hurry of flight, Aiken must have dropped. On his arrival at the house he dispatched a servant after his father-in-law, who was at Col. Miller's, telling him to hurry home—that Young Burton had been killed down by the field. It is proved that *no one passed up the road, from the time of Burton's passing down, and after Aiken dispatched the servant after his father-in-law.* He fled that night.

"A reward of $1,000 has been offered for him. We trust he may be apprehended. There can be no question of his guilt, or we should be silent. We know the duty of the press under ordinary circumstances, but when a deed is perpetrated, so foul and unnatural, and upon one who was so innocent, whose noble heart cherished no malice towards the dastardly assassin, and, when shot down, thought himself as secure as if by his own fire-side, we should be wanting in the discharge of what we deem our duty did we not appeal to every good citizen to use his utmost efforts in bringing to justice this *foul fiend* in human shape."

Fent seemed to have no doubt at all. "'... no question of his guilt...' The *News* would not have printed Dr. Aiken's name unless it were certain. They said as much. And the evidence was so conclusive. I suppose it just shows how little we can read a person's heart from the outward appearance," she sighed. "What did the writer call him?" She looked again at the newspaper and mouthed the words: "foul fiend in human shape." "Just right," she said aloud as she began folding her letter for mailing.

13

BILL HYNSON'S BOLD STEP

Monday, December 13, 1841

Bill Hynson looked at his rifle and fretted. He didn't know whether he ought to keep powder in the pan or wait until he was ready to shoot. *It shouldn't be too long*, he thought. He needed to be ready, because he would get only one chance. The rifle was already loaded, so he only had to pour powder into the pan, which he did, thinking once again that he ought to give up this antique and buy a caplock rifle. He laid it gently on a chair and inched the window up in its sash until there was room to aim and fire down into the street below.

Preparations completed, Bill sat down on the floor so as to be out of the view of any casual observers who just happened to look up at the second story window. The only danger lay from the outside, because the two people working in the store today were up front where they could see down the street. There weren't any customers, because everyone in town was down at the courthouse. He had slipped up here without being seen, he was sure. He wasn't sure that he would be able to escape after it was over, but that was the chance he took. Phil would have done this—had talked about doing it—if he hadn't come down with a fever that put him in bed delirious. Bill would do the job for him. He was a Burton by marriage now, and that carried some responsibilities. Maybe with Aiken dead everything would finally begin to get better. Maybe Rosalie would stop crying and smile again.

Bill clenched his teeth in anger. He could be hanged for what he was about to do. It just wasn't fair. Unless the jury was very sympathetic, he would at least be sent to jail. Maybe hanged. *Aiken deserved to die, if anyone ever did,* he told himself again. Justice was supposed to be done by the courts, and here Aiken was about to be set free. Andrew Porter, the editor of the newspaper, had told him so just yesterday. Andrew, a native of North Carolina, had just been here a little over a year and had recently become publisher and editor of the *Batesville News,* when William Byers, the founder, decided to go into political life. Porter was studying law and planned to be admitted to the bar, so he probably understood the politics of the Aiken case better than most. "Not enough evidence," Andrew had said.

Bill took out his wallet and pulled some folded newsprint from it. He unfolded the large article that had detailed the inquest's testimony and smoothed it on his knee. He re-read the article. "Not enough evidence!" The words burst from Bill's mouth, despite his need to be quiet. "How can they say that?"

Well, Bill had all the evidence he needed. Aiken would get justice this morning, even if it was from his rifle instead of the end of a rope. No matter what the consequences. He owed it to Nick. And to Rosalie. How did that line go? Something about she couldn't love him unless she loved honor more? Today was the day of his honor, and Nick's.

How had it come to this? he asked himself again. Aiken was a clever man, that was sure. The man had been hiding out in Saline County not far from Little Rock—"visiting friends," he said. He claimed he had heard that the sheriff was looking for him back in Batesville, so he had turned himself in at Little Rock. The sheriff there took him into custody and sent a deputy with him to deliver him to Batesville, but Aiken apparently acted like a completely innocent man, eager to cooperate. They said that he and the deputy rode into town without irons, with his rifle in its holster, the picture of a man returning home. The only good thing about that, Bill figured, was that Dr. Burton didn't have to pay anybody the $1,000 that he probably didn't have.

That was about two weeks after Aiken killed Nick, Hynson recalled. Sheriff Engles didn't treat him as an innocent man, at least at first. He took him from the deputy and put him in custody at Engleside. *Like a guest!* For his protection, Engles said. Then for three days the sheriff and Tom Johnson, the judge of the circuit court, had had a parade of witnesses to come to his house and testify before them and Aiken. The general public was kept out, and the sheriff said it was his right, because it was just an investigation, not a trial. Everybody figured that it was the same information that came out at the inquest. After that Sheriff Engles formally arrested Aiken for murder, and put him in jail. But everybody knew that didn't make sense. The sheriff must have learned something that would convince a jury. But those who knew weren't talking. Bill separated out another creased scrap of newsprint torn from the *News*, a small one from Nov. 11 and nervously stroked his goatee as he read it again.

> **Dr. Trent C. Aiken**, charged with the murder of *Nicholas E. Burton*, was apprehended on the Allum fork of the Saline, and brought back to this place. His Honor Judge Johnson, after an examination of witnesses, which occupied three days, committed him to jail for further trial.

They had all thought it was over then—a little wait until the Circuit Court convened in December, then a quick trial and a hanging. And Aiken knew he was caught. Word had gotten around that after he was formally charged, he and his wife had sold his four slaves to Captain Bean for $500. Hynson figured that was just a gift from his father-in-law for lawyer fees—and, he'd bet, running money if it came to that.

But then strange things had started happening. First the rumor had gone around that Aiken was living at home. Then he was seen riding into town surrounded by a group of men with rifles. When Fent Noland had asked, the Sheriff told him that he had turned him loose on his word—until the Circuit Court convened in December Aiken could go nowhere but his home and inside the town of Batesville. Seems the jail was too small for a long stay, and Aiken must have put up a large bond to get himself in house-arrest. Neither Bill nor any of his friends had ever heard of such a thing.

Bill had to admit that Aiken had not run. Probably couldn't afford to lose whatever bond he had put up. But what sort of arrogance was it that made Aiken ride around town like a free man? Dr. Burton had seen him ride by on Main Street one day, and several men nearby had had to restrain the doctor from running out to confront him. Everybody he knew was angry, even Rosalie, when she wasn't crying. Bill opened the last of his clippings and read it over. It was from the December 2 issue of the *Batesville News*. The editors quoted a note from Absalom Pike's Whig newspaper in Little Rock, the *Arkansas Advocate*, followed by their own outraged comment at the reality of Aiken's treatment.

> "Dr. T. C. Aiken, charged with the murder of Nicholas E. Burton, was apprehended on the Allum Fork of Saline, carried back to Batesville, and committed to jail."
>
> We clip the above from the *Advocate*.
>
> Reluctant as we are to say anything touching this matter until it shall have been determined by the laws of the land, our duty as the conductor of a public press compels us to correct the above so far as the "jail" is concerned. Dr. Aiken has been ever since he was committed, at a public Tavern, living on the fat things of the land, enjoying the society of his friends, and as we are informed retaining his weapons.
>
> We know not where the Sheriff gets his authority, neither can we conjecture his sense of propriety in permitting such a state of things.

Bill crumpled the newsprint in his hand in irritation. Outrage got no one anywhere, though. The sheriff just commented that things were under control, and that the court would dispense justice. Even so, it was noted by everyone that Aiken went nowhere without his bodyguards, Rangers volunteering their time to keep Cap'n Bean's family safe.

Finally the Circuit Court began to organize what everybody recognized would be one of the great sessions in Independence County history. Starting on Monday, Dec. 6, depositions were taken, which took several days.

The court itself started on Tuesday with the selection of members of the grand jury and their dismissal to their private chamber. Their task was to hear testimony and consider whether or not they would indict people charged in various cases. As it happened, Aiken's case was the most celebrated, although there were several others, including assault and battery cases against Dr. Burton for his attacks on Mr. Carter and Mr. Estabrook, and one each against Bill and Nat Hynson for fights they had gotten into in debating the guilt of Aiken.

Judge Johnson was a young man, for a judge, and he was thought to be fair man, with a good head for the law. He appointed William Denton prosecutor, which was a good sign, because Denton was Noland's law partner and could be expected to pursue the Aiken case with vigor. Nothing was heard from the grand jury as they went through their cases, so the court went on with its postponed cases, lawyer's appeals for new postponements, and other such business. Those other affairs of court, however, were deemed minor by the public, as they waited to hear what happened in the grand jury deliberations.

That gathering amounted to a separate court hearing, and their isolation was frustrating to the general public who filled the Public Square around the courthouse. The grand jury had been sent to an empty mercantile store fronting on the square. The place had been quickly reorganized into a jury room as far as was possible by moving the showcases and other furniture not fixed to the floor. A few benches had been brought in and set up facing the tables in the front where the lawyers and fourteen jurors sat. When room for the witnesses was created in front, there was not a lot of room remaining for the benches, so most of the public was excluded from the proceedings. The glass windows in front, however, afforded glimpses of the interior for the few who could find room to cup their hands around their eyes at the glass as they peered into the chamber.

The major sensation was caused late Tuesday afternoon, when the few observers who were fortunate enough to have found seats in the room came out to report on Trent Aiken's own testimony. At the request of the grand jury and with the concurrence of the lawyers, Aiken had been called to the front to speak for himself. The observers reported that the doctor had walked to the witness chair as if he had no intention other than trying to be of service to the court. Asked by the prosecutor to explain his absence from the county for two weeks after the shooting, he spoke clearly and calmly. According to the composite account pieced together by the observers at the tavern later, Aiken's testimony went like this:

> That morning I was looking for a strayed heifer below my house. I heard hoofbeats on the road across the bayou. I couldn't see the road from where I was, but I asked my boy who it was. Richard told me it was Nick Burton headed north at a steady pace. I went back to my search and soon found the heifer. As I headed her back toward the barn, I thought it might be a good idea to talk with Nick about his father. I thought if I could get him to understand my side of the argument, he might be able to help the doctor see things more reasonably. I saddled up my horse and went up the road, telling the boy where I was going. I rode for about an hour, but I never caught up with Nick. I realized that since I didn't know where he was going, I had no way of knowing whether he had turned off the road. So I gave up and headed back home. When I got back I went in the house for dinner.

A while later I decided to go down toward the valley and go hunting. I took my rifle and walked a ways without seeing much of anything. I heard a shot from over toward the road, so I thought I'd go see who was shooting on our land. I didn't see anything until I crossed the bayou and got to the side of the road. Just a little way down from where I was I saw a body lying in the road, with a horse standing over under a tree. I went to see whether I could do anything for the man, but when I got there I saw the wounds and knew that he was dead, When I turned him over I saw that it was Nick Burton, and I knew I was in trouble. I saw some horse tracks heading on down the road toward Batesville, so I figured people would be coming soon. Since there was nothing I could do for Nick, and it looked like a murder to me, I headed back toward the house.

By the time I got there, I had come to a conclusion that I didn't want to have to deal with Dr. Burton until he had calmed down. I figured he would be so upset that he'd probably shoot me before I could say a word. I have some old acquaintances from Tennessee who live down below Little Rock on the Saline. They keep asking me to come down for a visit. I decided that would be a good time to make that visit. I sent a boy to tell Jesse to come home from the Millers'. I packed up a few things and explained the situation to Jane and her mother. When Jesse got there, I told him my plan. I said I would be back in a few weeks, when Nick's death would be a thing of the past. I deliberately didn't tell him where I was going so that he wouldn't have to lie if somebody asked for me.

I went on down to my friends' place on the Saline. I settled in with them and did my best to make the visit pleasant. There was no news from Batesville at all, even though I got hold of the Little Rock newspapers every week. Finally I saw a notice that the sheriff was looking for me, and I read that Dr. Burton had set a prize of $1000 for finding me. Just like I figured, Burton was going to make me the killer. I decided that I needed to get back here, but I needed to worry about my safety. I went to the sheriff in Little Rock and "surrendered." I explained the situation to him and asked him to send me back to Batesville with a couple of deputies for protection on the way. He gave me one deputy, and I got back safely and told Sheriff Engles my story. The rest you know.

According to the observers, Dr. Burton had interrupted several times with shouts of "Liar," and when Dr. Aiken finished his statement, Burton leaped to his feet and said, "You killed my boy!" When the room came to order, the attorneys for both sides asked questions of Dr. Aiken, but his testimony didn't change, and the grand jury dismissed him at the end of an hour. The other witnesses, the observers said, were all the ones who had testified at the coroner's inquest, so nothing new was presented.

The grand jury went into closed session for their deliberations, so there were no longer any observers to report on the discussion. Apparently the panel had continued on down their docket through Wednesday, because there was no report from the grand jury given to the court at all. The general knowledge was that all attempts to wheedle information from the jurors, who were allowed to go home at night, had failed. The sheriff or the judge, or both, had apparently threatened them with jail for contempt, and they weren't about to say anything until they reported to the court.

There was still no news by Thursday, Dec. 9, so the *Batesville News* had had to go to press without anything to say about the indictment. By nightfall, however, there was a rumor being passed around that the Byers brothers, William and John, together with John Miniken, had bought forty acres of farm land from Trent and Jane Aiken that very day. Everybody found it vaguely significant, but no one seemed to have a plausible theory to explain it. Maybe they needed more money to pay more lawyers for the trial before Aiken finally got strung up. Or maybe the Aikens were getting ready to run.

At last the grand jury came back in on Friday, but to everyone's frustration they spent the day reporting on the minor cases. Dr. Burton had had one assault and battery case dismissal and one indictment; the judge had found him guilty and charged him $25 and costs. The Hynsons were found guilty and had to pay $10 and costs on each count. No jail time for any of them, they were relieved to see. The court adjourned for the weekend, and, of course, there was no other topic of conversation in Batesville. Dr. Aiken was at last going to be indicted, and they could all move on toward the inevitable outcome.

This morning, however, was for Bill a Monday of gloom. Andrew Porter's earlier prediction drummed in his head: "not enough evidence." Then the moment came, and Porter was right. To great uproar, the grand jury had reported that Aiken's murder charge was "not a true bill." *They did not indict! There would be no trial! Aiken was a free man!* Bill stood in stunned silence for a moment, shocked to the core despite his advance warning from Porter. He turned and left the courthouse with new resolve. Now it was time for justice. *When the courts fail, the citizens must act,* he thought grimly.

For some time people had been walking up the street from the courthouse, indicating that for many of them the important part of the session was over. Bill could think of no reason for Aiken to hang around. He had been turned loose, and he and his family would probably feel safer if they could get back out to the Bean place. So they should come by soon.

And there they were. As usual, the doctor was surrounded by his bodyguards, while the Beans, Aikens, and Millers were riding along behind. It was going to be a tricky shot. Bill rose to his knees, lifted his rifle, and rested the muzzle on the sill of the window. It wouldn't do to stick it out the window and tip them off what was about to happen.

The procession moved slowly up the street, and people were coming out of buildings all along Main Street to look at the most notorious man in Batesville on that day. To Bill's amazement, the crowd pressed close to the wagon and horses, some shaking their fists at Aiken. The Rangers moved to surround Aiken's horse with their own to keep the crowd away. They moved almost in front of Bill's second story window, and he sighted down the barrel. He discovered that he was not high enough, and the men surrounding Aiken kept bobbing in front of Aiken in his sights. He still thought he could make the shot, however, but he belatedly realized that if he shot, there was no telling who would get hit. Even if he got Aiken, the ball would likely go through him and hit someone in the wall of flesh that was so tight around the entourage. He couldn't do it.

Slowly he took his hand off the trigger and pulled the rifle away from the window. He sank down on the floor, overwhelmed by the sense of failure. *I've lost my chance!* A wave of shame passed over him. He had messed it up. Any other man –Phil, Fent, his brothers—would have found a way to do it right.

There was nothing more to be said. He had failed!

He looked out the window again, just in time to see the Aiken party turn at the intersection and head down out of sight to cross the bayou.

Nick was dead, and Aiken lived. The anger and Rosalie's tears would continue.

14
JUSTICE DENIED?

December 10, 1842

The familiar wing chair was so comfortable that William Byers was forced to admit that just leaning back in front of the fire in the company of his family was a pleasure that he had missed for months. Now that he was back from Little Rock, perhaps he could slow down and rediscover the joys of being at home in Batesville. Being elected a representative to the General Assembly was flattering, and it did give him an opportunity to see life from the viewpoint of the capital—the sort of perspective John Ringgold and Fent Noland had had through the years—but it tended to take over your life, at least while you were at the Rock.

William Byers had studied law and had been admitted to the bar at Mount Vernon, Ohio, where he practiced briefly before coming to Batesville, but he had never before been in political office. After leaving the *Batesville News*, he resumed his law practice. He and fellow Whig Beniah Bateman had been elected to the General Assembly for the 1842-43 session.

He was glad to be home, and his family was delighted. The two boys needed to have him around, and the girls were his special comfor. This homecoming was certainly more pleasant that that of a year ago, when he and his family had returned from a trip back to Ohio just in time for the death of Nick Burton and all the unpleasantness that followed.

Things had changed a great deal in the year since that tragedy. The Burtons were scattered. Dr. Burton had moved to Little Rock to build a new practice. Bill and Rosalie Hynson were happy in their new house and were building a family. With the birth of little Emma this year, it looked as if Bill was finally settling down. He had bought out the interest of both of his brothers, so he was now the sole owner of the mercantile store. With the failure of the lime factory, Nat and Anna Hynson had returned to Chestertown, probably to her pleasure, Byers thought. Henry Hynson had long had other ventures at hand, so Bill became the store's owner. He was striving to collect the debts owed the store, a process that included suing his own father-in-law, the thought of which brought a smile to Byers' face. He wished he had heard that conversation between the doctor, Rosalie, and Bill. Emily Burton Wilson was still living in Mississippi, and her sister Mary Weaver lived near Philadelphia.

Nannie Burton, the youngest daughter, had married Edwin Burr last December at her sister Mary's home in Pennsylvania; everyone had thought it best for them simply to get out of Batesville for the event, since it was just weeks after Nick's death. The newlyweds had long since been back, and they seemed to be prospering. Burr was an energetic young man from Massachusetts, and he had both the financial backing and the drive to become a successful businessman in Batesville. Burr had bought the house the Burtons had lived in, and he and his wife were living there now that the Burtons were gone.

Phil was still in the area, living with the Burrs, but he was trying to build for himself a life in the mercantile world. He was talking about going into partnership and opening a store, but he was not sure he would stay in Batesville.

The stone catafalque planned and bought by the Young Men's Meeting had been carved. It had been erected, with the Burtons' permission, over Nick's grave, and it was striking. It resembled a large stone table, and it had no decoration at all, just the name, "Nicholas E. Burton." Nothing more. It was unique in the graveyard, and it would do what was intended—call attention to the tragedy of his young life lost.

Byers had had a year to think about what had happened in the case of the death of young Nick Burton. He still did not know what had really occurred. He personally thought that it was possible that Trent Aiken did kill the boy, but he was not sure, had never been sure. The Burtons and Hynsons, and even Fent Noland, had been sure, and still were, as far as he could tell, but he needed more convincing.

Despite William Byers's relative youth—he was 32—he was, after all, a lawyer, and he had been a newspaper editor. Byers prided himself on being the sort of professional man who is careful in his judgments about matters of evidence and law. The evidence against Aiken was purely circumstantial; any lawyer worth his salt—and not blinded by emotional involvement—could see that. The grand jury members had done what they had to do. If they had indicted Aiken on the basis of what had been presented to them, they would have been derelict in their duty. The *Arkansas Gazette*, which was, to be sure, a Democratic paper, and therefore likely to be biased in favor of Aiken, had said it bluntly: "...the testimony produced against him, at the late term of the circuit court of Independence County, not having been sufficient to justify the grand jury in finding a bill against him." That was clear to him, and apparently it had been clear to Henry Engles. It was not so clear to the Burtons and the Hynsons.

Beyond the weakness of the evidence, though, there was the troubling problem of motive. A lot of people seemed to be willing to believe that Aiken would be happy to shoot a boy to strike back at the boy's father, but Byers found that a very hard pill to swallow. How could any reasonable person think that way? It may have made sense in ancient times or as an Italian family feud, but not in the modern world. Byers had no doubt that part of Burton's vision of the motive was Aiken's refusal to accept his challenge to a duel. Burton had certainly been willing to proclaim that Aiken was a coward for refusing, and Byers was convinced, even though he had never gotten the doctor to say so, that Burton thought that anyone branded a coward would be willing to do any sort of back-shooting to get revenge.

Byers did not accept that. He knew that some would say it was because he was from Pennsylvania and Ohio, but he found it repugnant to have a duel to settle disputes or redeem honor. For years—some said because of the death of Alexander Hamilton in a duel in 1804—people in the eastern states had found dueling increasingly unacceptable. While it continued in the professional military, it became a distinctively Southern custom for civilians. Many social leaders in the South, Byers had learned, had fought duels, whether willingly or unwillingly. In Arkansas it still flourished even though it was illegal, and Byers was sure that it contributed to the national image of Arkansas as a violent society. While those duels, even the fatal ones, tended to be legally overlooked locally, there could be national consequences, as when Andrew Scott, judge of the Superior Court of Arkansas Territory, was refused reappointment by the U.S. Senate in 1827 after he had killed a fellow Superior Court judge in a duel.

Byers wondered what Fent thought of that. He did not know what perception a more mature Noland had of his own duel, but he did know that Noland had served as a pallbearer at the funeral of J. J. Anthony, a legislator who had died in a knife fight on the floor of the Arkansas House, and Fent was outraged over the incident. Burton, however, continued to regard dueling and the code of honor as the keys to understanding a man's character, and that had apparently led him to conclude that Aiken was capable of an act of cowardice like Nick's murder.

Despite his misgivings, the fact remained that Nick had indeed been shot in the back. What explanation could there be? Would they ever know what had happened? If Aiken had been mentally deranged at the time, it had not been permanent, for Aiken had acted in very normal ways since he had been discharged by the court. He was cautious, of course, because both Dr. Burton and Phil were known to be eager to see him dead, and no one could assess the degree of danger from them. Aiken usually went to town with several friends or Rangers to provide security, and he was circumspect about where he went and at what hours. Still, he was a doctor with a practice, so he had to visit his patients, even with some risk.

In Independence County, Byers knew, there was no unanimity as to Aiken's guilt. It was not just a matter of inadequate evidence or an unclear motive. There were a great many people who believed strongly that Aiken was an innocent man. The veterans of Bean's Rangers might be expected to be supporters of Jesse Bean's son-in-law, but the unshakeable belief in Aiken was far more widespread than among just that group. In fact, Byers had observed, those who were convinced of Aiken's guilt seemed to be concentrated in Batesville and members of the Whig party.

Aiken and Jesse Bean and John Miller were leaders of the Democrats, the majority party in the county. Byers saw that it would be possible to interpret this whole affair as a political feud, Whigs versus Democrats. Yet he was certain that it was not political. It had begun with men, not parties. Even so, it was hard to deny that now, a year later, the sides had hardened into camps identified by political persuasion.

That may already have been true at the time, though. Byers recalled vividly the anguished discussions among the Burtons and Hynsons, and others, as to what had happened in those grand jury meetings. They referred frequently to their notion that some of the members of the jury, who should have voted against Aiken, had weakened and "gone along" with the other members. The grand jury consisted of sixteen men, with William J. Hassell as foreman. Byers knew that at least five of them were Whigs, and there might be more than he could identify. The accusations on the part of the Whig group were probably political comments about Whigs who were thought to have "given in" to the Democrats on the jury. Although he had not pursued it, Byers felt certain the reference was political, and that suggested to Byers that there was some feeling that the grand jury decision came down to a question of Whig loyalty, at least in the minds of those who believed Aiken was guilty. And that was not good enough for Byers, at least when it came to the legal process. Guilty was guilty, regardless of the defendant's political leanings, and the law was the law.

Byers believed in the legal process, as he had demonstrated during the last year. He and Trent Aiken had wrestled in the circuit court over a suit Byers had brought against him for debt. They had just recently settled the debt, and the case had been dropped. Byers felt good about that, not only because he had gotten a fair settlement, but because he had shown the community that everyone could return to normal and treat Dr. Aiken the way his discharge by the court entitled him to be treated—as an innocent man. But he knew some of the community never would.

At that point in his reflections, Lucy suddenly and noisily brought in the children to say goodnight to their father. Byers beamed, and all the dark memories vanished from his mind as he was buried under his warm, squirming, giggling children.

15
A DEPARTURE

December 27, 1843

Jesse Bean was ready to die. He had done all that he knew to do. The witnesses to the final codicil to his will had just left his house, leaving him lying in bed looking at the paper with all the signatures. It was his brother-in-law John Miller who had caught the weakness in his will, if it really was one. Jesse Bean doubted that this kind of caution was really necessary, but you never knew what would happen once grandchildren grew up, and once lawyers came into the picture. The codicil made it clear that it was his intention that all of the slaves would belong to Jane during her lifetime, then pass to the children of Trent and Jane. The house on Poke Bayou would likewise belong to Nancy for the rest of her life, to Jane and the children thereafter. John Martin and Bill Miller had come by at his request to witness the document, and now it was done. He could die knowing he had done what he could to take care of his family.

He had written his main will back in September of 1841, when he first began to feel sick. He had added the first codicil a month later. He winced at the memory—he was at John Miller's house signing that codicil when Nick Burton was shot, the event that had caused so much unhappiness.

It was like a curse. Look at what had happened since young Burton was killed. Joe Pentecost, having left the editorship of the *Batesville News* and become city clerk and treasurer, had died unexpectedly at the age of thirty-four. The three-year-old daughter of Henry Byrd had burned to death. Byrd was an outstanding painter who had been living here for the last few years doing portraits for all those who could afford him, like the Whig bunch in Batesville—the Ringgolds, the Nolands, the Byers family. His daughter's death had undone Byrd, and he had taken his unhappy family to Little Rock. There would be no more portraits done in Batesville. At about the same time, last spring, Henry Engles, who had not been re-elected as sheriff, was found shot to death. Even though he had understood that probably no sheriff could have survived the Burton business politically, he had taken the voters' desertion very personally. He was also a major loser in the closing of the State Bank, but so were a lot of other people around Batesville. His death was called a suicide, and people didn't talk much about it.

Fent Noland had begun to appear visibly ill, and some said they thought it looked like his consumption was getting worse. Bean was not surprised. 1842 had not been a good year for the Nolands' health. Fent had gone to New Orleans early in the year, but he had returned to Batesville in spring very ill. In May he spent three weeks in bed. As he had done before, he eventually rallied, gained strength, and resumed his usual activities. By last fall he had recuperated enough to travel, He and Luty had gone to Virginia to visit his family. They had a carriage accident there, and Luty was hurt. They returned to Batesville late in the year.

And I'm not going to be around much longer. Just a few months earlier Trent Aiken had listened to his chest, looked at the blood he was coughing up, and shook his head. He gave him medicine for the pain and told him to get his affairs in order. "It *is* like a curse," Bean thought. "Nick Burton will have plenty of company out there in the public graveyard."

Bean hoped that his family would not join Nick there any time soon, but the fact was that Trent and Jane had learned to live like hunted people, constantly in danger. They expected a shot out of the bushes at any time, and they never went to town unless some of the "guardians," as they had come to call them, were available to go with them. Living in the expectation of death—or the curse—had taken a toll on them, and he could see that his sweet-tempered Jane had become bitter. "And she had a right to," he thought with a surge of anger.

"What kind of people are these?" he asked for the thousandth time. "They know Trent. They have seen the good work he has done as a doctor. They have seen what a good family man he is. Why would anybody follow the thinking of that crazy Patrick Burton? He's just a bully," Bean thought. "I've stood down more than a few of that type in my time. They need whipping to bring them to a right mind, and some of them just need killing." Burton's attacks on Trent seemed to have had a lot of influence on some people. Trent's practice had fallen off some before Nick's death, and in the last year he had lost a lot of patients.

"Particularly in town," he thought. "Those damned Whigs! I wouldn't give a dollar, not even a State Bank dollar, for any of them. Well, maybe Ringgold, maybe Byers. I don't know what happened to Fent Noland—he used to be a friend. But the whole assault on Trent as the murderer had come from that Whig bunch. They stuck together. They could never carry elections, but they were sure of their platform."

Bean was pretty sure that the State Bank disaster could be laid at their door. The State Bank had finally been liquidated by the legislature the previous year, and plans were made for the various branches to go into receivership. For their part, of course, the Whigs blamed the Democrats, and they said that most of them were crooks. He did have to admit that William Ball was a major embarrassment for the party. The Fayetteville branch of the State Bank had never recovered the missing funds from the embezzlement case, and the state lost more than $46,000 to the missing cashier. Some claimed it was just politics, but it was a kind of politics he didn't like.

Bean had a coughing spell, and Nancy came in with a glass of water. He drank it and the coughing died away. "Want me to sit with you a while?" Nancy asked.

"No," he said with a reassuring smile. "I'm fine. I just get myself fired up thinking about the Whigs."

"So do I, Jesse, but don't let them kill you. You've been through all that. Rest easy." She mopped his forehead with a cool wet cloth, then left the room drying her hands on her apron.

The Whigs weren't going to have to kill him, he thought. He knew he was dying, and fairly soon. "Sometimes you just know when it's your time. I can't complain. I've done a heap of living." The silent phrase reminded him of Henry Ellsworth, the Indian Commissioner who had toured with him out in Indian country back in 1832. Both Ellsworth and Washington Irving had enjoyed the way he talked, especially his frequent use of "heap." They sat around talking with him just to laugh at his stories and his way of putting things. "Easterners!" he chuckled. His laugh brought on another spasm of coughing that subsided after a few minutes. He didn't mind being thought a strange character by Eastern folks. That was who he was, and it wasn't who they were. He *did* mind dying in his own bed coughing his lungs out, though, bleeding and burning up with fever. That's not the way a man should go. He had missed several more appropriate deaths earlier in his life, and he was grateful for that, he supposed. But they would have been closer what he thought of as the right way for a man to die.

He had missed some good chances to die right. The battle of New Orleans was one. The Seminole War in Florida was another. He fought hard for Andy Jackson and came home after both without a scratch. After he and the other people in the new states west of the Appalachians put Old Hickory in the White House, he had waited for a letter ordering him to do something else fit for a man of action, but the call didn't come until ten years ago, when the president had picked him to go keep the peace in Indian country. He had raised a good company right here in the county, and except for a few who died of diseases, he had brought them all home in good condition with a lot of grand stories. And they had stood by him through the Burton business. Most of them had volunteered to ride with their rifles at the ready when Trent and Jane had to go to town. "Good men," he thought with pride. Bean could have died at any time during that year on the prairie—there had been enough Pawnee arrows to do it, and there had been animals that could've done the job, too. But he had lived to return home from that journey.

He let out a long rasping sigh. He had lived through all that, only to go through the outrages of the Burton business and die in bed of bad lungs. At sixty he couldn't complain, but it was not the right time to die. He feared for Trent and Jane without him. For one thing, he was not certain the guardians would keep on helping when he was gone. They did it for him, not for Trent, and he didn't think they would keep on being bodyguards even for John Miller. And without the bodyguards, who knew what might happen? Phil Burton was still around, and Bean was not sure that he had ever given up on his hatred of Trent. And he had been told that Bill Hynson had even tried to waylay Trent after the grand jury freed him in Batesville. Who would have thought he had it in him? Maybe a rumor, maybe not.

He had already made Trent and Jane promise that after he was gone, they would leave Arkansas. There were plenty of other places where they could live well, and they wouldn't have to watch their backs all the time.

But it was still just a plain truth—they needed him. He was their best protector, and this damned thing in his chest was going to take him away. He sat up in bed and put the final codicil to his will on the table by his bed. The movement started his coughing again, and he heard Nancy's steps heading toward the bedroom.

"How did I ever marry as good a wife as she is? She's ended up more my nurse than my wife." He wondered, not for the first time, if she would marry again. He hoped so. She deserved more out of life than his money and an empty bed. "Well, it's not my choice and it's out of my control." He lay back on the pillow and prepared his smile for her entrance.

16
A MEETING ON MAIN STREET

Monday, May 15, 1848

Trent Aiken checked to see that his rifle was loaded and the cap was set before he slipped it into its boot on his saddle. All it would need was cocking and firing. Jesse had seen to it that he had a good caplock rifle and knew how to use it. But he really wouldn't need it. Those days were past, he felt certain.

He helped Jane up to her sidesaddle, then mounted his own horse. Normally when they went into town they took the wagon, because they usually had to haul groceries and other truck back with them. They were on their way to visit the Millers today, though, and Aiken wanted to return quickly, because there was a baby due south of their place in Greenbrier Bottom, and he wanted to be available when the time came. Jane never minded riding on a horse, even when pregnant, as she was now. Her father had insisted that she be a good horsewoman, and she was. She missed her normal armful of child, however, because she had usually had a young child to worry about and she felt easier if she had the baby with her, both for feeding and for maternal care. The children weren't really babies anymore, though—little Jesse was two—and they could safely be left at home in the care of their grandmother. The child she was carrying inside wouldn't be born for some months yet.

Aiken had heard some of the gossip that charged him with hiding behind his family, always holding a baby or sitting close to Jane so as to make a good shot impossible. That was the sort of thing he had gotten used to, the malicious gossip that emanated from "that Whig bunch," as Jesse Bean used to call them. The only positive thing in that little piece of fiction, he had often thought, was that while they were willing to murder him, they would draw the line at killing his wife and children.

To his surprise he had found that he missed Jesse almost as much as Jane did. He had genuinely liked his father-in-law, who was always full of wonderful stories from his action-filled life in the wars and on the frontier. Even more important for Trent, perhaps, was his great down-to-earth wisdom. Jesse always understood the real things, like how people were likely to act, what kind of villainy they were capable of, and how to protect yourself against them. All the sorts of things that Aiken never had grasped well. All his life he had been interested in healing, and medical practice had been a natural path for him to follow. And his life—his move to Arkansas from Tennessee, his marriage to Jane, his medical practice, his reputation in the community—had gone well, until that terrible day in 1841.

It had all begun with the death of that slave woman of William Byers. He had readily accepted responsibility, but it was the sort of thing that doctors had to live with. He had made the wrong diagnosis, and the woman had died. He was not certain that she would have lived had he chosen another diagnosis and treatment, but the fact was, she died under his care. He thought it was strange at the time, and ever since, that Patrick Burton had chosen to make a public issue out of it by attacking his professional ability. Doctors normally were more circumspect and kept such things within the fraternity, but Burton seemed to have no sense of professional propriety. And a challenge to a duel? He was a doctor, not a politician. If Burton thought that was the proper way to have a medical discussion, he would find few in the medical fraternity who would care to play his game. And then that outrageous circular Burton had printed up—what could anyone make of that? It could have had no other purpose than to destroy his career as a doctor. Why? Aiken had never understood. Never would.

But he had learned a great deal of the dark ways of the world by the time of the shooting. When he saw Nick's body, he knew it would mean trouble for him. Dr. Burton was capable of anything, and if the finger were pointed at him, Aiken wouldn't live to come before a jury. Jesse had agreed with his decision to leave town until things settled down and the situation came under control. He had taken off that night, and he had returned at the right time. He was charged, but Sheriff Engles had seen the weakness of the case against him and had been lenient on him while they waited for the court to convene. It had been the sheriff's idea to arrest him so that the case would be examined by the court. He had said he couldn't answer for the consequences if he just turned Aiken loose.

He was right. "That Whig bunch" had been furious anyhow, when the grand jury didn't indict him. Jesse had been careful to see that the Aikens lived like people under a death threat, cautious in their movements, escorted everywhere. Before he died, back in January of 1844, Jesse had made him promise to leave the area and not to let anyone but the family know where they had gone. Jesse always insisted that Dr. Burton was crazy, and he anticipated violence from him.

Things had changed a lot since Jesse died. Shortly after his funeral, Trent and Jane, obedient to their promise to Jesse, had sold their holdings in Independence County and moved to Mississippi, while Nancy remained in the old home up Poke Bayou. William Moore, whose sister Clara was John Miller's wife, had been a close friend of Jesse's. He and Nancy had been named co-executors of Jesse's estate in the will. Trent and Jane were relieved and pleased when Nancy Bean married widower William Moore a year after Jesse's death. She had sold the old place and moved to Moore's home in Greenbrier south of the river.

Dr. Burton had moved to Little Rock, and Phil Burton, who had vowed vengeance for his brother in the passion of the moment, had moved to Lawrence County. A few years later he had returned to Batesville, however. He entered a mercantile partnership and was selling dry goods on Main Street. Just the previous week Aiken had seen an ad in Fent Noland's new Whig newspaper, *The Batesville Eagle*, for the Shaw & Burton store "at the double Portico, on Main Street."

A lot of the people involved in the original troubles of seven years ago had died. Several of the Batesville lawyers had died. Mort Baltimore, the official coroner in the case, had died in Little Rock, where he was serving as a member of the House representing Independence County. James Pope, a lawyer who had married the daughter of Whig leader David Walker in Fayetteville before moving to Batesville, had died. A month after Pope's death in 1845, William F. Denton, Noland's former law partner, died in Batesville of "black tongue" contracted from the damp courthouse floor.

Henry Hynson had lost a son, his wife, and a daughter in a four-month period in the winter of 1845. Only a month after the cold and wet burial of young John Hynson, John's mother Eliza Magness Hynson died at age 34 of pneumonia contracted at the funeral, and her nine-year-old daughter Elizabeth died six weeks later. Henry was now living with his oldest daughter's family in Batesville. The Hynson childrens' deaths were not isolated ones. On Oct. 25 of that year, Trent Aiken remembered, his friend Robert Williams had written a letter to his brother John in Ohio in which he mentioned the "sickly season" in Batesville at that time:

> We have lost some five or six of our very best citizens in town, and quite a number in the country... George Case lost one of his children a few weeks ago. We have a disease prevailing here this season which comes on by a chill, and sometimes the persons never revive, but go off in twenty-four hours; but generally the chill is succeeded by fever which goes off in eight or ten hours; the next day another chill and fever,

and in this chill the patient dies. When medical aid is called in early in the disease, no difficulty is expected in raising the patient.

Bill and Rosalie Hynson had moved to New Orleans, and they had lost a child in an accident in Dr. Burton's back yard in Little Rock during a visit in 1847. Lawyer William Byers had spent years building a fine new house northeast of town, not far from John Miller's house. Unfortunately, his wife Lucy died suddenly at the time they were just moving in 1846. She was buried in the public graveyard near Nick Burton's grave and catafalque. William Byers tried to assuage his grief by erecting over her tomb the largest memorial yet placed in that cemetery, a marble obelisk that bore on it the names and dates of Lucy and the two deceased children, Sarah Vesta and James, who were buried in Ohio.

In the last year had come another major event, even though life in Batesville continued without significant change. The United States had declared war on Mexico and had launched an invasion. The outcome was the extension of the United States to include a third of the old country of Mexico, and a lot of people were talking about going west to newly American California. Batesville had sent two companies of cavalry to the war under the leadership of former governor Archibald Yell. Both Yell and Andrew Porter, the former *Batesville News* editor who was commander of one of the Batesville companies, had been killed at Buena Vista. Porter's body had been returned to Batesville and had been buried beneath a large obelisk erected with public donations by the Masonic lodge to which Porter had belonged. It stood in a new cemetery at the northeast end of Main Street, which had been extended in that direction by several blocks while the Aikens had lived away.

All of these rapid changes in Batesville and in the lives of the principal actors in the Burton tragedy, had convinced Trent Aiken that it was safe to return, freed by time from his promise to Jesse. In Mississippi, Jane had found that she missed her mother greatly, which was no surprise to Trent, considering that she had never lived apart from her parents before. She also needed help with the children, and Nancy had made it clear in her letters that she would like very much for the Aikens to move back with her grandchildren. Just a few months earlier they had moved in with Nancy and William in the Greenbrier area.

Everything had gone well, but then they discovered that Bill and Rosalie Hynson had also returned to Batesville, as had Phil Burton. Bill now seemed to be a serious family man, though, and Phil was in a business partnership, running a mercantile store, and appeared to be doing quite well. Phil had not married, but he was twenty-seven years old and was a mature, settled man. He was frequently out of town on business in Lawrence County or Little Rock, and he appeared to be a man of affairs. Aiken had tried to have a conversation with both men, if only to ascertain where they stood, but he had not been successful. Phil Burton had just said bluntly to him that they had nothing to say to each other and that he never wanted to see Aiken again. When Aiken tried to talk with Bill Hynson, he had merely turned away from him in his store without speaking. Aiken had abandoned attempts to heal the breach, but he did not anticipate further problems from either man, as long as he was cautious and did not offend them.

By the time Trent and Jane had crossed the ferry and were riding down Main Street, he could tell she was a bit tired. They had crossed at the old Ramsey ferry downriver from the town rather than the Greenbrier ferry, because they wanted to ride down Main Street before going on out to the Miller farm by way of the new bridge over Poke Bayou at Spring Street. They were thinking of moving back to Batesville, and they wanted to look at the houses that were being built on the extension of Main Street.

It was in the School Addition, called by that name because it belonged by federal law to the county for the purposes of education. It had been platted and lots sold back in 1842, and there had been a good deal of investment in the extension of Main Street, primarily for the purpose of building residences.

The Aikens had noted on their return that the Methodist church and public graveyard, which had stood on the outskirts of town when Nick Burton was buried there, now were surrounded by houses. Batesville's original plat had early proved inadequate for the number of people who wished to build town houses, and the original town plat had become the business district. The difficulty in expanding up Main Street was the coincidence that the location of Batesville placed the original town just west of Section 16 of the township, which was reserved by federal law for the use of educational institutions. Recognizing that any educational system stood to benefit from the sale of town lots rather than country acreage, the town decided to plat out the section, which became the School Addition, and offer it for sale as part of Batesville, the proceeds going to the schools by way of a special board.

Jane revived a bit as they discussed the impressive homes on upper Main. Having visited in the house before, they could talk in detail about the elegance of the central hall house built by George Case for the Williams family, the first to be constructed in the new addition. They had heard that the Presbyterians, who had been organized since 1842, were hoping to build a church right on Main in the last block before the School Addition began. The Aikens were pleased that Batesville was finally adding another church, even though they themselves were Methodists. As they rode along, they speculated on where they might want to build their new house.

As they reached the courthouse square, everything looked familiar to them, because there had been few alterations in the last decade. The names on the stores were different, of course, for businesses had changed hands fairly frequently in the hard times since the collapse of the State Bank, but the buildings and the bustle of people remained the same. After the State Bank went into receivership in 1843, the imposing bank building had stood empty until it was sold at a sheriff's sale in 1846 to William Byers. He was slowly turning it into an office building.

The couple reached the dock area at the foot of Main, then turned around to begin their ascent back up the street to buy some goods at the mercantile store before crossing the bridge over the bayou. The Aikens saw several friendly faces, and Trent greeted them with a smile and a tip of his hat from the back of his horse. After passing the courthouse and the Ringgold home, they came in easy sight of the impressive former State Bank building. Across the street, Spit Corner was inhabited, as usual, by several men sitting and talking on the benches. Trent was startled to see Phil Burton step out of the shadows on the board sidewalk of E.T. Burr's store into the dusty street in front of them. Burton, well dressed in his business suit, looked handsome but lean, with dark circles under sunken eyes. Phil stood there staring at him, and Aiken thought it was finally time for that conversation. Then he saw the shotgun that Phil was holding along his right leg, and he realized that he was wrong, that he had been wrong all along.

Aiken saw Phil's shotgun come up, and he reached desperately for his rifle in its scabbard, but he never got it free. "For Nick," Burton said in a low, clear voice. And fired.

The blow knocked Aiken from his horse, but because of the pain in his stomach, he barely felt the blow as his back struck the ground. He knew he was gut shot, but how badly he was unable to tell, because he didn't seem able to move. As the darkness closed in, the last thing he saw was the stricken face of Jane.

17

A NEW LIFE

Saturday, September 15, 1849

The bile rose in her throat, and she could taste its bitterness. Jane Aiken had never really known hatred before, even through all the early years of the Burton affair, so she was unprepared for the strong passions that flooded through her body, shutting out all other emotions, and even thought.

The problem was, she didn't really know whom to hate. Phil Burton, that smooth-faced man who had plotted for years to avenge his dead brother? His lunatic father in Little Rock? Trent, for trusting these people? The "Whig bunch," who were walking around Batesville with an air that now everything was fine, that justice finally ruled?

She felt a constant rage, and it was consuming her. She did not even care, because she felt that the whole series of incidents had already destroyed her life, her happiness. "They have taken everything from me," she thought. For the first time she understood the passion for vengeance, which she had thought belonged only to men in their peculiar makeup.

She had already felt that passion when she saw Trent lying in the street. She had felt it as she got help for Trent. That passion had sustained her as Dr. Chapman did his preliminary medical care, putting a salve on the wounds, covering them with a bandage to stop the bleeding, and giving her a vial of painkiller for Trent when he awoke. The passion had given her strength to get Trent into a borrowed wagon for the trip home.

It had begun to lessen somewhat, fading into the background of her mind as she ministered to Trent. He awoke in pain, but after Dr. Chapman came and removed the buckshot from his stomach, Trent had begun to feel better. Dr. Chapman had said it would be a painful recovery, and he was forthright that there were a lot of things that could go wrong before Trent was out of danger.

Her desire for vengeance was abated somewhat when she heard in May that Phil had been indicted by the grand jury for assault with intent to kill. She did not mind that he had been released on a $2000 bond put up by John Ringgold and Hulbert Fairchild, the lawyer who had bought her old home, the Bean place, now named "Sunfish." Phil Burton would come to trial for shooting Trent. With good care, perhaps Trent would be strong enough to testify against him. If he was not well enough to get to the courthouse, at least he could give a deposition to be read. Either way, at last he would have a chance to tell his side of the story. And Phil would spend some time in jail to think it all over, a punishment he richly deserved, she felt as she watched Trent try to deal with the pain of wounds that stubbornly refused to heal.

At the June term of court there had been a motion to continue the case to the fall term of court. Burton was trying to get depositions from people who were no longer in Batesville, probably, William Moore thought, because his lawyers were going to try to argue that the shooting was justified by Trent's having killed Nick. So Phil was going to try to turn the case into the trial that the grand jury had denied seven years earlier. "Fine," she had said to her mother. "We'll just see how this turns out when Trent has his say."

But Trent did not get his say. He died on June 20. The damage was too great, Dr. Chapman said, and infection had set in, despite all the care she had given him. She watched Trent slip away, first into delirium, then into coma. The children said goodbye to their unconscious father and helped keep the vigil. Trent Aiken's breathing became so shallow that no one was quite aware when it stopped. Then her rage returned. It had been calmed again in September when the court convened, but the case was postponed once more, this time until March.

In March the prosecutor replaced the "assault with intent to kill" charge with "murder." The grand jury, with Joe Egner as its foreman, had no difficulty bringing in an indictment for murder against Phil Burton. A jury was selected, but then Burton wanted to get a deposition from Peter Engles, who was not in Batesville. Frustratingly, once again the case was postponed.

At least the judge did not give bail, and the widow took some pleasure from the fact that Phil Burton sat in the small brick jail alongside the courthouse through the hot summer, waiting.

Finally the case came to trial, and the arguments were long and complex. Contrary to Jane's expectations, what happened in the courtroom was not simply dealing with the shooting, but all sorts of wide-ranging explorations of Phil's motive, which opened up the question of whether Trent had murdered Nick. Judge Scott had done his best to contain the trial, but it was a lawyer's case, not a simple judgment case. As the judge made rulings against the defense on procedural issues and admission of evidence, they lodged objections to his rulings and made them part of the court record—eight "bills of exception" in all. William Moore explained to her that it was to lay the groundwork for an appeal when Phil was found guilty.

But he wasn't. This morning the jury had retired to consider, and in no time at all, it seemed to her, they returned. "Not guilty." Phil Burton was discharged, and the County was ordered to pay the court costs.

Not guilty? When half the town had seen it? "Justifiable homicide," they claimed. Which meant it was all Trent's fault. Which meant that Phil was right to have killed him. Which came down to one chilling reality for her—not only was Trent dead and his killer alive, Trent had been labeled a murderer for all time by the court. There would never be another opportunity to clear his name.

And politically, she knew, nothing would ever be done. Her cousin, Bill Miller, who was clerk of the circuit court, had political aspirations, and he had explained that his public support of Trent was very costly, because many people across the state thought Trent was guilty. He had told her he needed for Trent to be exonerated by the trial, for then he could continue his support. Otherwise, he said, he would have to back away. Well, now he would. So Trent had no more friends. It was all over, and Trent had lost. Her children's father was branded a murderer.

All that was left for her was to deal with her rage, but she knew it would never go away. The only answer she could see was to leave the area. She would miss her mother and William Moore, of course. But it would be no sadness to her if she never saw the people of Batesville again.

She was still a young woman—widow, she corrected herself. She had children to raise. She needed to leave, get on with her life. She knew she was not going to continue the fight. No matter how much she felt like killing Phil Burton herself, she would never do it. For one thing, it would accomplish nothing. Burton's death would bring back neither Trent nor his good name. For another thing, she had children who needed her, and a jailed mother would ruin their lives. She was also wise enough to guess that killing Phil would not kill the hatred she felt for them all. She suspected that hate and bitterness were feelings that would become her permanent partners, no matter what she did.

She would leave this town, this state. Go west, maybe. Into the new America beyond the plains. Wherever she went, however, she knew she would long for the death of Phil Burton. And continue to curse the Burton name.

18
OLD FRIENDS

December 31, 1857

Joe Egner knocked on the front door of the once-elegant brick Ringgold house, now usually vacant.

I hope he has a fire going, he thought. It was a bright day, but it was cold, and he shivered beneath his greatcoat. He had not noticed whether there was smoke from any of the chimneys as he walked down Main Street. Had he looked, he was sure, he would have seen smoke at least from the chimney of the kitchen out back. He had sent his servants Peter and Diannah to take care of Fent while he was in town, and they were completely trustworthy. They would already have fed Fent his breakfast and seen to it that he was dressed for the day.

Fent was so thin and frail, though. Egner had been shocked at his appearance when Noland got off the steamboat three days earlier. He looked much older than his forty-seven years, and he was coughing into his handkerchief again. He may not get much older than he is now, Joe had thought in a sudden realization. Batesville's literary giant, still a young man by Egner's standards, was probably going to die soon, betrayed by the weakness of his body.

Just as Joe raised his hand to knock again on the door, he heard the fumbling at the latch. The door swung open, and Fent was there with a welcoming smile on his face.

"Come in, Joe. It's a pleasant day, and I'm glad you included me in your morning schedule." Noland was dressed informally, in a smoking jacket with no neckscarf and open collar, an indication that he had no immediate plans for leaving the house. "I see that it's still a bit chilly out, though," he said as he shook Egner's hand. "Come in and sit by the fire. I'll find something to drink to take the chill off."

Egner allowed himself to be pulled into the hall, smiling with genuine pleasure at Fent's strength and enthusiasm. "I'll pass on the drink, thanks. Nice to see you so fit this morning, Fent. You must have slept well last night."

"Oh, I suspect it has more to do with having had an excellent meal with old friends," Fent said with a broad smile. He had dined for the second night in a row with the Egner family, and he had been unusually entertaining. He had regaled the table with stories of Pete Whetstone, his bucolic hill character who still wrote letters telling of his adventures. As the family members around the table broke into frequent laughter, Joe had noticed that even the house slaves were standing close on the other side of the door to hear Fent's humorous monologues in Pete's voice.

"I hope that's true, Fent. You certainly did your best to make it an excellent evening. I'll be hearing about Pete Whetstone for a long time. How has your morning gone?" Joe asked as they seated themselves in front of the small fire in the fireplace in the parlor.

"It's been productive. I have Peter boxing up some things for me to take back to Luty in Little Rock, and I have almost finished the financial accounting, at least as much as I can do right now." He sighed. "John Ringgold would be so upset if he knew what a mess he left behind. I guess that would be true for any of us, though. When you don't expect to die, you don't keep things straight. There's always going to be time for that, it seems."

"You make me want to go right home and start straightening things up, Fent," said Joe with a thin smile.

"You have no need to worry about following John off the

deck of a steamboat, Joe. You already did that, and you lived through it. Remember? I guess that means you're immune. You're going to outlive us all." Noland well remembered the town's grief back in 1837 when Egner was thought dead in a steamboat explosion until he appeared in town a week later after a float down the Mississippi on a log.

John Ringgold, however, had died with no fireworks. He had just walked off the deck of a steamboat on the Mississippi in the middle of the night. That was in the previous July, and there was still no explanation of how such a thing could have happened. His body had been recovered a day later and sent back to Batesville for a huge funeral. He had been buried in the Batesville cemetery alongside Elizabeth, whose grave was not yet completely covered with grass. There had been a crowd of mourners far bigger than the small cemetery could contain.

Fent and Luty and their young son had moved to Little Rock two years earlier, in 1855, so they had to make the sad steamboat trip to Batesville twice, once for Elizabeth's funeral in 1856, then for John's just six months ago. Joe had not had much opportunity or time to talk with Fent, because there was always so much Ringgold family activity to keep everyone occupied. In fact, it was only during the fall visit of the Nolands that Egner had had a chance to visit personally with Fent. Luty had been much occupied with her sisters, both married and unmarried, trying to see that all living arrangements were made, the slaves parceled out properly, and the house prepared for closure. Fent, however, was administrator of his father-in-law's estate, and his task on that trip was to organize the complex financial picture of the Ringgold estate and see that all the necessary steps for the termination of John Ringgold's business ventures were taken in proper order. Egner had a good mind for that kind of thing, having long been a successful merchant as well as the Independence County treasurer, so he had made himself useful as Noland's assistant. Even so, the pressure of the business to be done had limited the time available for personal reflection and conversation.

Egner was glad that Fent, having finished with Christmas activities in Little Rock, had come back to try to finish up his administrator's work. He had planned for the two of them to find time to talk about old times. Last night's pleasant mood, together with Fent's unusual energetic affability, had led him to seek out Fent this morning. It was a time for reflection, he hoped.

"Will you be back this spring?" he asked Noland.

"If I need to, I guess. I'm anticipating that most things can be done by mail, and I'm counting on you for help from time to time—the things that require a personal look."

"You know you can count on me, Fent."

"I'm thinking about going down to New Orleans after it gets warm. I don't seem to be getting better, and I think it's time for another visit to my doctors down there. They may know of something new to try. More than Arkansas doctors, I hope. And the warmth may do me some good, too."

"Good idea."

They sat in companionable silence for a while, staring into the fire.

Now's the time, Egner thought. Striving to be casual, he asked, "Do you ever think about Nick Burton?"

"A lot," Fent said. "Whenever I think about Batesville, which is every day."

"Do you ever see Dr. Burton in Little Rock?"

"Every so often I catch a glimpse of him, but we never speak. We really don't have anything to say to each other. I suspect we are each a reminder of Nick and Phil for each other, so we'd just as soon not cross paths. He's married again, you know. He's starting a new batch of children." He grinned at Joe. "Seems funny that some of us have such a hard time having just one child, and others can breed like rabbits."

"Hey, is that a personal attack? Oh, you're referring only to the good doctor," Joe said with a smile.

"Yeah. And I think he may be turning into 'the *good* doctor.' I haven't heard of any temper explosions at all since I have been in Little Rock, and that's a town that enjoys its gossip. I hear only good comments about him, and he and his wife are active in social circles. Maybe he's a changed man."

"Maybe the whole Batesville affair has burned out some of that anger. I'm sure that by now he must see that the whole storm revolved around him and his temper, not around Nick."

"I'd like to think he sees that," Fent agreed. "Without his rages, would the tragedy have happened? I often replay the whole thing in my mind, like going to the theater to see the same play night after night, wondering whether the plot will change. Will it come out a different way?"

"That's interesting that you say that, Fent. I do the same thing. I've thought through several different versions of the play. I've ended up with a version that I can't get out of my mind. It's not any happier, but I think it's what really happened." Egner paused to gauge Noland's reaction.

After a moment's silence, Fent repeated, "What really happened." He waited a bit, then looked at Egner. "Well? Tell me your story."

"Are you sure you want to hear it, Fent? You may not find it to your liking."

"Now you've really made me curious. " Noland turned toward Egner. "I'm not a fool, Joe. I know you have never been happy with the story the way it worked out. I know there are some unsolved mysteries in it. Whatever you've put together, if it may get us closer to the truth, I want to know it. I can take it, old friend. Don't sell me short."

"I'm sorry, Fent. I didn't mean it that way. You have a temper of your own, you know, and sometimes I want to be sure I'm not arousing it."

"Don't worry. If your version helps me understand Nick's death, I'll be pleased, whether I like it or not."

"All right, then." Joe leaned back in his chair and put his hands behind his head, facing the fire. "You're right. I have never been happy with the story, because there were some things that just never made much sense to me. Like why anybody would shoot likable, goodhearted Nick to begin with. Like why Aiken—or anyone—would shoot a boy to get even with his father. Like why the whole county could disagree so strongly on Aiken's guilt, when they've all got the same facts. Something always seemed wrong to me about the basic story.

"I used to talk about this with Henry Engles, you know. I wish he were still with us, Fent. I would like for him to be here with us talking about this now. He agreed with my reservations. When he talked with Dr. Aiken after he came back from the Saline, he believed Aiken was telling the truth. He said Aiken just did not seem like a murderer trying to lie his way out of it." Egner shook his head, as if to set aside his memories of the long-deceased Engles.

"Anyway. As I thought it through, I decided I would set aside the notion that Aiken killed Nick and look at the other possibilities." Egner held his hand open, preparing to strike the points off on his fingers. "First, there could have been a madman—your favorite idea, except you think it was Aiken—who just happened to be there in the woods wanting to shoot someone, and Nick just happened to ride by. Could happen, I guess, but that explanation belongs with the Aiken theory. It's really the same one, just with an anonymous madman. I don't find it any more satisfying.

"Second, there could have been somebody stalking Nick for a reason. Somebody who had followed him out of Batesville—remember that very few people knew where Nick was going that morning. By the time he knew that Nick was going on up the bayou road, he would also have figured out that Nick would be coming back the same way, so he didn't have to do anything but hide in the woods and stay put until he saw Nick coming back. It's pretty unlikely that a seventeen-year-old would be sent off alone on some errand miles away that would take more than just that day. So that would explain *how* it could happen.

"The key to that possibility is that someone had to want to kill Nick. Specifically Nick. And no one ever came up with any enemies for him. No schoolboy grudges. No trouble with a woman. No irate husband. No reason to think that he had anything worth stealing. So why would anyone go to all that trouble to kill him? It doesn't sound very reasonable after all.

"Third possibility. Somebody shot Nick by accident. If a hunter were out in the woods and fired at a target and missed, what would happen to the shot? It could happen. I've seen hunters, including me, take shots at deer, quail, ducks, squirrels that missed; those shot could have gone anywhere. Nobody is very careful about what's behind the game they're aiming at. He could have hit Nick and gone on his way without knowing what he had done. If he figured it out later, after he heard about Nick's death, he wouldn't be likely to step forward to own up to it.

"The problem with that possibility is that there were eleven shot in Nick's back and head. I finally got a chance to talk with Jesse Bean about that. I figured that he was about the best hunter that I knew of around here. I asked him what he made of the eleven shot. He said that it was impossible to be real sure about what it told you. There was only one shot, he said. He was pretty sure the buckshot were from a single load. More than that, he couldn't be sure, because the size of the shot pattern depended a lot on the amount of powder that was loaded, the number of the shot, and the distance. Every hunter did his own loading, so unless you saw the load, you couldn't be sure what was there. Without knowing any of those things, he said, you couldn't figure the others. I pressed him to give me his best hunch about the shot in Nick's back and head. He said that probably the most important thing was the fact that Nick looked good in his coffin. If he had been shot point blank, there might not even have been a head left. Uh, sorry, Fent. But that's what he said. So he thought that the shotgun was probably fifty feet or more behind him and just the edge of the scatter caught Nick. So that pretty much rules out a hunter so far away that he didn't even know he had hit anyone with his shot.

"That leaves us with just one possibility, it seems to me."

"Bonaparte Allen," interjected Fent.

"Bonaparte Allen," agreed Joe. "The fourth possibility is that the sole witness pulled the trigger. Remember, the only description of the killing that we have is Boney's. So if he did it, we have no trustworthy account at all. Without his story, we have nothing except a shot heard by Bean's slave boy and a body with buckshot in it in the road.

"The question that leaves us with is whether it was deliberate or an accident. For a deliberate shooting you need a motive. I could never come up with a reason for Boney to want Nick dead. I even thought about some problem involving Boney's wife Julia, but when I thought about Nick's busy town life and her busy life as a wife and mother in the heart of the Allen clan south of the river, I decided that was just too implausible. And that left me with an accidental shooting." Joe sat silently staring into the flames.

"How would we ever find that out?" asked Fent. "The only way I can see is to confront Boney with your possibility and see what he says. But he and his family went to California a while back, just before Luty and I moved to Little Rock. So we'll never know what he might have said."

"You're right. It's too late to ask Boney now. But what do you think of my reasoning?"

"I wish you had told me your thoughts long ago, Joe. You make a good case, I'll grant. I see several problems with your story, though. And you have to admit there's still the Aiken possibility, which still seems to me the right one. All you have against that is the feeling that it doesn't make sense. I wonder if there are not a lot of things in this world that are true, but don't really make sense."

"I'm sure you're right, Fent. It may be that we're not supposed to make sense of a lot of things. But I don't like that idea very much. I want things to make sense. I like for things to fit my experience. That's all I have to go on."

"I do the same, Joe. I think maybe we put the emphasis on different kinds of experience, though. I'm pretty good at reading people, and I saw—still see—a guilty man in Trent

Aiken. His character was flawed. A coward, a frightened man on the run, maybe a little crazed. Maybe Dr. Burton pushed him over the edge, but it was Trent who pulled the trigger. No, Joe. Aiken was our man."

"I didn't see that man, Fent. I saw a fine man trapped in a net of suspicion he couldn't handle. I thought everything Trent did was consistent with his being an innocent man." He sighed. "We both saw the same things, so I guess we interpreted them to make sense to us in our different ways."

Egner leaned forward to look into Noland's face. "Let me ask you a question. If my reasoning is, well, reasonable, what stops you from considering my conclusion? Is it that you don't want to accept the consequences of that outcome?"

"You mean the fact that if Boney did it, then Aiken didn't? That Aiken must have been telling the truth all along?"

"And that Phil Burton killed the wrong man. That Jane Aiken became a widow with five children for no good reason."

"No. I don't like those implications. If your theory is right, there are too many victims." He ticked them off on his fingers. "Nick, Trent, Phil, Jane and the children, Phil's wife, Dr. Burton, the Burton girls."

"And truth and justice, Fent. Don't forget them."

"And truth and justice. And that's too many victims, Joe. So, since this is all just theory, I choose not to believe it. Let sleeping dogs lie."

"That's your choice, of course. I only raised these questions in the interest of truth and justice, but we believe what we wish." He sat looking at Fent through a long silence before he spoke again. "I should tell you one more thing, though."

"What?" Fent asked sharply.

"It *is* too late to ask Boney Allen about all this now, and he'll never come back from California. But I decided to ask him before he left. I just couldn't stand not knowing, or at least not even asking. So I did."

"And..." Fent said, as if the word were a tooth being pulled from his mouth.

"He broke down and confirmed the theory."

"Oh, God. Is that true?"

"That's what he said."

They sat quietly for some time, staring into the bright red embers. Egner watched Fent out of the corner of his eye. He saw no movement at all. Noland sat as if carved of stone as the story rearranged itself in his mind. Finally he leaned back in his chair and turned his head toward Joe. "Tell me the rest," he said quietly.

"Boney said that they were going to fire his shotgun a couple of times so he could give Nick some tips about leading birds. Nick went on down the road toward the open field, saying he would try to flush some quail. A rattler crossed the road under Boney's horse; he reared and Boney's shotgun went off. Nick fell dead. Boney said that he raced into town to get help, but he knew it was too late. He decided on the way that he didn't have to tell; 'a shot out of nowhere' would get him out of trouble and couldn't hurt Nick. Besides, he said, he was terrified of Dr. Burton. He stopped and hid his shotgun under a fallen tree, then went on into town.

"He said he almost told the truth when he got to Dr. Burton's office, but the doctor was so furious that he had left Nick on the road that he almost strangled him on the spot, so he lost all courage in telling the true story of the accident.

"Boney said he got worried when Dr. Aiken was accused. He claimed he would have confessed if there had ever been any danger, but he figured the courts couldn't hurt Dr. Aiken because he didn't do it. Sure enough, the grand jury refused to indict. They understood there was no evidence worth going to trial with. So Boney figured he was in the clear and it was all over.

"He cried when he told me what it was like when he heard that Phil had shot Trent Aiken. When Trent finally died a couple of months later, he was so distraught, he said, he thought about taking his own life. He didn't because of his own family, but he decided to leave Arkansas forever. When he got the opportunity to pull up roots and head west, he got his family ready to move. That's when I visited him to ask my questions."

"You didn't stop him? You didn't demand that he tell people?"

"What would be the point? Boney wasn't guilty of anything except fear. He shot Nick by accident, and none of the rest happened by his intention. It's like he pulled the trigger that started a set of dominoes falling. He didn't set up the dominoes, and he pulled the trigger by accident. So what would be the point of a public announcement at this late date?"

"What about removing the stain from Trent Aiken's name?"

"Who would care? Jane and the children, I suppose, but I have no idea where they are now. I don't think she wanted us to know where they are. I think she has moved to a new life and isn't looking back.I don't know that she would be grateful for more turmoil about the Burton case."

"Shouldn't the Burtons know the truth?"

"Why? Dr. Burton lives there in Little Rock. You can tell him the story when you get back to the city, if you wish. I doubt that he will choose to believe you. He probably would be the one most condemned by the true story, and so he will choose not to believe it.

"The same goes for the Burton girls here. Nothing will change for Emily, Rosalie, and Nannie, except to feel even worse about the whole story, and maybe to begin to hate Batesville. Besides, what do we have to tell except a theory? I have no evidence. I just know what I know."

"So you and I know the truth. Does anyone else?" asked Fent.

"Boney, but he's not telling."

"And we have the truth, and we're not going to tell. This isn't right. I was wrong, and I ought to confess it to somebody."

"I know. I'm not sure about keeping my mouth shut, either. But I can't help but think your conclusion is right—let sleeping dogs lie."

Fent was silent for a while. Egner waited. "I guess there really isn't anyone *to* tell, now that I think of it. So many people involved in the story have died, or moved. It's already part of history. Not many people want to look back, so I guess this is the end of it."

"Yeah. Unless you want to tell Luty. Or Dr. Burton."

Egner stood to leave. Noland slowly got to his feet, like a tired old man. He looked at Egner and slowly shook his head. "You've kept this to yourself for a long time, Joe. You sure know how to keep a secret."

Egner gave a slight shrug before turning away. At the door he stopped and took Fent's hand. "Are you glad I told you, Fent?"

"Yes. No." He sighed. "I don't know." He looked away and said in a shaking voice, "I'll never be the same. But thanks, Joe." He opened the door for Egner, who stepped down to the front yard. "You know, Joe? One thing I'm glad of, is that Phil went to his grave without knowing that he had killed the wrong man."

Egner turned back from the front steps. He looked at his frail friend for a moment, then decided to lie. "Yeah. That's a good thing. See you tomorrow." He walked up the street.

At the corner, Egner looked back and waved at Fent, who was still staring at him from the open door.

19

A BEDSIDE VISIT

July 8, 1851

Phil Burton was dying.

It came as no surprise to him. He had had consumption for several years now, and he knew of no one who had ever escaped the disease in the long run. It was that realization, that his life would be short, that had spurred him on to shoot Aiken three years earlier. That, and the pleasure of completing the mission that had given his life meaning ever since he had promised his dead brother and his living father that he would kill Trent Aiken. It had taken years of waiting, but he had done it.

As he lay on his bed in his room in his sister's house, still called "Engleside" even though the Burrs had owned it for several years, waiting for death by coughing, he reflected that he had no regrets. The love and devotion shown to him by his sister Nannie, particularly through the last few months of this disgusting illness, reassured him that she had no regrets either. Nick had been avenged, and all the Burtons were pleased about it.

Poor Father, Phil thought. His sons are slipping away. Selden, his first born, didn't really count, because he was a grown man, a doctor, and he had never even been to Arkansas to visit. Nick was gone, and he would be soon. But his father still had four wonderful daughters, Phil thought. He pictured Mary Weaver in Pennsylvania, whom he had not seen for years and would never see again. Rosalie Hynson and Nannie Burr were here, of course. And so was Emily, finally. Her husband George Wilson had died in Mississippi, and she had come here to live, bringing her two children. A year ago she had married William Byers, who had been a widower with young children for too long. Emily was now the mistress of Catalpa Hall north of town, and he saw her frequently. Phil was surrounded by the three sisters he loved dearly.

He had taken care of his affairs as well as he knew how. He had virtually no estate left for anyone to have to deal with. A few months ago he had even spent $600 of his dwindling cash to buy twenty-year-old Priscilla from Bill Hynson, who needed money, then had turned around and sold her to Rosalie for "$1 and love and affection."

There was little more to be done.

There was a gentle knock at the door, and Nannie poked her head through to see if he was asleep. Seeing him lying there staring at the ceiling, she opened the door and came in. "There's someone to see you. I think you will be pleased, Phil. Shall I show him in?"

"Of course, Nannie. If you think best."

She disappeared for a moment, then returned with a man behind her. "Surprise. Here is Mr. Allen, come to see you." She turned to Boney Allen and took him by the arm. "You come right in. Phil's feeling fine today, and he'll be glad to talk with someone besides me. Can I bring you something to drink?"

"No, thank you, Mrs. Burr. I'm not going to stay too long."

"Well, I'll just leave you two to visit. Call me if you need me," she told Phil. She vanished, closing the door behind her.

Phil mustered a smile and shook the hand that Allen offered. He motioned to a chair against the wall. Allen picked it up, brought it close to the bed, and sat down.

"I'm pleased to see you, Boney. You were the last person to see Nick alive, and I can't think of anyone I would like to see more right now. I was surprised that you didn't come to talk with me during the trial. I thought you more than anyone would be pleased to offer me congratulations."

"That's what I came to talk to you about, Mr. Burton, uh, Phil. I wanted to talk to you about the shooting of your brother."

"Do we still have things to talk about, Boney? Aiken has paid his debt, and the whole affair has finally come to an end. It's over." He looked distant as he said in a quiet voice, "I will see Nick soon, Boney, and I will be able to tell him it's over. I did what I promised him."

"Please. I have come because I heard that you don't have long." Phil was startled to see Boney's eyes brimming over. He was touched, because they had never really had any connection other than Nick's death. "I feel that there are some things I need to tell you while there is still time." And with that, the tears spilled down his cheeks, and he buried his face in his hands.

"Boney, it's all right. I am reconciled to my death. I have no fear."

Boney raised his head and wiped his eyes with his sleeve. "You don't understand. There are things you don't know." He trailed off and seemed paralyzed, looking at the floor.

"I'm at a loss. Just say what you want to say, Boney."

In a strangled voice, Boney said, "I killed Nick."

There was a long silence. Finally he cut his eyes toward Phil to assess the effect of his statement, but all he saw was a man in paralysis, staring at him. Allen looked back at his hands in his lap. Suddenly it was as if a log jam had broken, and the words began to pour out. "I didn't mean to do it. It was an accident. The way it happened, Nick and I had been talking about hunting all the way down the bayou road. By the time we got to Dr. Aiken's road we were talking about quail hunting, and Nick said he had never done that. I was talking about how hard it is to react to the birds breaking cover in time, and how hard it is to lead them just right so you can take them down. Nick wanted to see how that was done, and he kept at me to take a shot with my shotgun. I told him that it was loaded with buckshot and would tear a bird to pieces, if I was lucky enough to hit one. But he kept on at me.

You know how he was when he got excited about something.

"Well, I finally agreed. I thought a shot from me, and then one from him, might be an interesting thing to do, we had had such a good time together. I told him that we needed dogs to flush the birds, but he said he could do that. I stopped in the road to get my shotgun out and ready to fire. I had just filled the pan and cocked the flint back when I spoke to him and realized that he had gone on a ways down the road toward the field ahead of me. Just then a rattlesnake came out from the side of the road, saw my horse, I guess, coiled and rattled. My horse skittered sideways, you know how they do, and I lost my balance. I heard my gun go off, and I regained my balance just in time to see Nick landing on the ground alongside his horse. I rode up and saw his head all bloody. When I saw that his eyes were open I knew that there was nothing I could do for him, so I just hit a gallop out of there as quick as I could, heading for Batesville."

He stopped, out of breath. There was a long moment of silence. Phil, frozen, finally asked in a whisper, "Why did you not tell anyone?"

Anguished, Allen said, "I was going to. But I looked back and never saw anyone around, and on my ride back I knew that it would be just my word that it was an accident. There weren't any witnesses. And I knew your father would kill me. You know what he's like. I wouldn't have lived through the day. It was an accident!" He paused.

"I still might have told," he said more quietly. "But when I told your father about Nick he started choking me just for running away from the scene. I thought I was a dead man then. I knew if I told him what had really happened, it would be the end of me. Nick would have forgiven me, I believe, but your father never would have. So I told my story without saying it was my shotgun..."

"Where *was* your shotgun, Boney?" Phil interrupted. "You didn't have a gun when we saw you in Batesville."

"I hid it in a brush pile along the bayou on my way back to town. I knew if somebody saw that gun, there would be too many questions. There are lots of people who can tell if a gun has been fired recently, too. So I got rid of it and went back for it the next day."

"And you played a role."

"I had to, if I was going to stay alive. I went back to the scene with all of you, and I saw the search everybody did. I saw the finger turn toward Dr. Aiken, and I almost told. But I knew that he was innocent, and there couldn't be any real evidence against him, so the law wouldn't do anything. I let it be.

"Then, later on, as people got more and more riled in Batesville, it had gone too far for me to say anything. Dr. Aiken, or some of Cap'n Bean's friends, anybody might have killed me for the trouble I'd caused. Or Dr. Burton might have killed me for killing Nick. When the Grand Jury refused to indict Dr. Aiken, I knew I had been right. It had cost him some money, and I was sorry about that, but he lived through it, and I lived through it, and it was over. Nick couldn't be brought back, no matter what we did.

"Everybody scattered after that, and I went on with my life, my family, raising crops, and my kids. I got religion, because I had a lot of sin that needed washing. When I threw myself on Jesus, I was cleansed. The preacher said so. But I never told anybody except Jesus. After that everything was fine, until you came back to town, and Dr. Aiken came back. I should have told you the whole story then, but I thought it was all over. I didn't think there was any need to. I never thought you would shoot him. When I heard you'd done it, then it was too late." He sighed deeply, his voice quivering.

"I figure I caused Dr. Aiken to die, not you. And that's what I came by to tell you. At the judgment, when you get asked about it, you can say it wasn't you that killed him. It was me. When I die, I'm going to have to answer for it. But you don't have to. It wasn't your fault." Face wet with tears, Allen slumped in his chair, as if all of the words that had filled him had been expelled, leaving a collapsed body in work clothes crumpled on the chair.

Phil lay back slowly on the bed, his energy gone. He stared at the ceiling. He had no words to offer Allen. He wasn't even sure what he felt. He was just tired. Tired as he had never been before.

"Say something, please." Allen's words were a plea.

"I killed the wrong man," Phil said in a whisper, staring at the ceiling.

Allen nodded slowly, agreeing. "Can you forgive me?" he asked plaintively.

Phil was silent a long time.

"It was an accident." Allen's words were just a whisper, a plea.

"No. Just go away."

Allen stood up, looking at Phil, who just stared at the ceiling. After a moment, Allen turned, shoulders slumped, and stumbled toward the door. He turned back toward the bed, wiping his wet face on his sleeve. Phil had not moved. After a brief silence, Allen opened the door and went out without another look.

A few moments later Nannie came in, having shown Allen out. She was not her usual bubbling self, because Allen's silent and somber departure, he had opened and passed through the front door before she could even get there, had left her troubled.

"Well, Phil. It was good to see Mr. Allen, wasn't it? Did you have a good visit?"

"I'm going to sleep now. I'll see you in the morning." Phil turned on his side, looking at the wall, without another word. Nannie, now even more troubled, said "Good night, Phil," and kissed him on his unresponsive cheek. She stood looking at him, indecisive, then left.

Phil Burton never said another word, and no one ever saw him awake again. Two days later he died.

He was buried alongside his brother Nick in the public graveyard, together beneath the catafalque. The Burton sisters had the stonemason come to the cemetery. There, he followed his instructions: in letters matching the "Nicholas E. Burton" at the head, he carved on the foot of the flat stone table the words "Phillip P. Burton."

Nothing more.

AUTHOR'S NOTE

As is appropriate for one of the oldest towns in Arkansas, there is an active group of local historians who have for decades collected and published historical documents and written excellent historical studies of the colorful past of Batesville and Independence County. Most of the documents about the Burton case can be found in the fifty-year run of the Independence County Historical Society's *Chronicle*, as well as so much of the collateral history that informs the antebellum background I have included in the narrative. Many of the documents and relevant artifacts are contained in the Old Independence Regional Museum, so the researcher has materials at hand to pursue the case.

The documents contained in this book are real: Anna Hynson's two letters, newspaper accounts, court records. I have merely quoted them with minor editing. Without providing all the documents, I have tried to present the evidence as it is known from the real sources.

The people are also real, although I have attempted to supply their thoughts, speech, and aspects of personality that cannot be known from the documentary evidence. In no case have I sought to belittle any character; I have tried to follow the patterns of behavior and supply motivations and thoughts that seem appropriate. I hope that I have not caused offense to descendants, but there is always that risk in interpreting history. After much wrestling with the issue of whether to change the names, I decided to keep the historical ones. I hope that others will become interested in this story—and in Batesville's fascinating history in general—and that they will pursue the historical evidence into the documents. My keeping the real names is an attempt to encourage those pursuits.

I have made concessions to the modern insistence that words should have only one correct spelling: I have standardized the spelling of several names, despite the 19th-century's relaxed approach to orthography. Thus Dr. Aiken's name is spelled in the original documents as Akin, Aiken, and Aikin; in this book it is Aiken. The sheriff's German name was properly spelled Engels, but it appears in many sources as Engles. I have standardized it and his home, "Engleside," to reflect the contemporary spelling.

As for the rest—my descriptions, my characterizations, my conversational usage, my interpretations of their thought and behavior—all are open to challenge and re-interpretation. I will welcome such a response, because that is the way the past should be treated. We humans make many decisions in the light of our understanding of the past, and we need to be energetic in continually reassessing our interpretation of it. Our history is always being researched, re-analyzed, and re-negotiated in the present by historians. That process, though, should not involve just professional historians. The rethinking of our past is an endeavor for all of us as humans. To the extent that we think as historians—people making sense of the past—to that extent we are exercising our *humanity*.

The tragic death of Nick Burton is therefore a relevant event for anyone trying to understand the human condition. It is particularly important, though, for those who live in Arkansas and in Batesville, for it is a significant window into a past that has produced our present. It is to those 21st-century citizens that this book is offered. I hope it may serve as a useful portal to the past.

George E. Lankford
Batesville, Arkansas

Appendix 1

Some Family Genealogies

Nathaniel T. Hynson IV = Sophia Ringgold   *(Chestertown, Maryland)*

      Henry Ringgold = Eliza Magness

      William S. = Rosalie Burton

      Nathaniel T. (5th) = Anna Medford

      Charles E.

John Ringgold = Elizabeth Sprigg   *(Maryland to Illinois to Arkansas)*

      Lucretia = C.F.M. Noland

      Sophia = William Stone

      Adelaide = R.G. Shaver

      Frances = A.C. Oliver

Joseph Sprigg Jr. = Ann Taylor   *(Maryland to Illinois)*

      Elizabeth = John Ringgold

      Lucretia = John Redmon = D.J. Chapman

      Maria Barbara = A. Baird

P. P. Burton = Emily Scott = Mary Shields   *(Virginia to Mississippi to Arkansas)*

Selden

Mary

Emily

Nancy

Phillip P.

Rosalie

Nicholas

SELDEN – Became a doctor, never came to Batesville.

MARY – Married Abram Weaver, lived in Pennsylvania, Mississippi and Memphis.

EMILY – Married George Wilson in Holly Springs, Miss., with children Frank and Nancy. At his death she married William Byers in Batesville.

PHILLIP P. – Never married, died in Batesville.

NANCY – Married Edwin T. Burr, lived and died in Batesville.

ROSALIE – Married William S. Hynson in Batesville; they moved to New Orleans and Little Rock. At his death she returned to Batesville and married Frank Archer.

NICHOLAS — Died unmarried in Batesville.

NOTE: These are only the children by Emily Scott; there were more by two other wives.

Appendix 2

Some Images from Old Batesville

C.F.M. ("Fent") Noland (1810-1858)

Courtesy of Historic Arkansas Museum, Little Rock

*This oil painting is the work of portraitist John Henry Byrd,
who lived and worked in Batesville during the 1840s.*

Lucretia Ringgold Noland (1822-1862)

Old Independence Regional Museum, Batesville

This oil painting is the work of portraitist John Henry Byrd,
who lived and worked in Batesville during the 1840s.

John Ringgold (1794-1857)

Courtesy of Independence County Historical Society, Batesville/
Old Independence Regional Museum, Batesville

This oil painting is the work of portraitist John Henry Byrd,
who lived and worked in Batesville during the 1840s.

Elizabeth Sprigg Ringgold (1803-1855)

*Courtesy of Independence County Historical Society, Batesville/
Old Independence Regional Museum, Batesville*

*This oil painting is the work of portraitist John Henry Byrd,
who lived and worked in Batesville during the 1840s.*

Batesville in 1840 (model)

Courtesy of author

Main Street in Batesville (ca. 1866)

Courtesy of Independence County Historical Society, Batesville/
Old Independence Regional Museum, Batesville

The Burton monument in Oaklawn Cemetery

Courtesy of author

The Burton monument was originally erected in Pioneer Cemetery on College Street in Batesville; it and the graves were moved to Oaklawn after it opened in 1872.

The Ringgold House (1827-1964)

Courtesy of Old Independence Regional Museum, Batesville

Catalpa Hall (1846-1952)

Courtesy of Old Independence Regional Museum, Batesville